COLD LEAD VERSUS A SILVER TONGUE

A new plan for escape suddenly came to him. Drawing hard on his cigarette, he expelled a mouthful of smoke into the bottle. Holding his thumb over the opening, he pulled at the cigarette again and repeated the process of blowing the smoke into the bottle . . .

"Jackson!" Rowdy put panic into his voice. "I've got a genie in here. In a bottle! Hurry! He's a mean one!"

"A genie!" Stonehead Jackson breathed. "You sure he's a mean one?"

"The ones in the brown bottles always are," Rowdy insisted. "Quick! Hand me your gun, and I'll shoot him as he comes out!"

DEAD END TRAIL

Avon Books are available at special quantity discounts for bulk purchases for sales promotions, premiums, fund raising or educational use. Special books, or book excerpts, can also be created to fit specific needs.

For details write or telephone the office of the Director of Special Markets, Avon Books, Dept. FP, 105 Madison Avenue, New York, New York 10016, 212-481-5653.

NORMAN A. FOX

DEAD END TRAIL

AVON BOOKS NEW YORK

AVON BOOKS
A division of
The Hearst Corporation
105 Madison Avenue
New York, New York 10016

Copyright © 1944 by Norman A. Fox
Published by arrangement with Dodd, Mead & Company, Inc.
Library of Congress Catalog Card Number: 87-91456
ISBN: 0-380-70298-3

First Avon Books Printing: May 1988

To
Sergeant Joe Fox,
my brother,
and to his outfit,
the Fourth Marine Division

CONTENTS

1. A Horse in the Hand

OF ROWDY DOW, sundry reward dodgers decorating blighted fence posts and gnarled stumps from the tortured badlands of eastern Montana to the higher ranges of the Rockies, said many things. They described him as standing five feet eleven in his socks and weighing one hundred and seventy pounds, and they attributed to him a pair of hazel eyes, a mop of black hair, inclined to curl, and an aggregation of features designed to make him a devil with the ladies—a most flattering statement. Also, they mentioned that he had taking ways, and listed the things he had taken, the cattle and moneys of more prosperous and prosaic people than himself. For his capture, they offered a sum large enough to excite the timidest citizen, and they hinted that Wyoming, Idaho, and the Dakotas had reason to sweeten the kitty. They stated his age as eighty-two, but this was obviously a typesetter's error as he was only twenty-eight.

These posters also presented the only picture that Rowdy had ever been foolish enough to have taken. A blemished likeness, it had been cut from a group photograph made when Rowdy and several friends of the long-riding gentry had visited a Chinook studio after a large evening of tipping the festive jug. The result was startling. It portrayed Rowdy as having a choirboy's face, but the angelic effect was offset by an exceedingly untidy cigar clamped in a corner of his mouth, and by the fact that he was wearing a stiff derby hat, donated by the photographer who had helped with the jug and thereby gotten into the spirit of the affair. Horses had been known to shy from that picture.

Of late, this likeness had again appeared in the public prints, this time followed by lengthy columns largely made

1

up from the imagination of newsmen who had found it impossible to contact Rowdy, a great fellow for travelling. These accounts had much to say of Calamity River, that unruly tributary of the unruly Missouri, and of a dam that had been swept away by a cloudburst, and of a wild ride down Calamity Valley, made by this same Rowdy Dow for the unselfish purpose of warning the scattered ranchers that their chimneys would shortly be submerged. Quoth the Butte *Bugle:* "If this act of noble heroism is to go unrewarded, a blemish shall have been placed upon the escutcheon of this fair state that will make unborn generations hang their heads in shame." The Billings *Breeze* was of the opinion that a bust of Rowdy should be placed in the state capitol, and turned Rowdy's picture over to a local sculptor after prodigiously passing the hat; while the Great Falls *Gazette,* a more conservative sheet, contented itself with referring to Rowdy as the modern Paul Revere.

Thus had Rowdy overnight become a public hero, and thus had a sceptical governor, prodded by a wagonload of petitions and numerous none-too-thinly-veiled threats of impeachment, granted him a full pardon. The pardon had been presented to Rowdy on the end of a forked stick when he'd been cornered by a posse in a box canyon and had forted up behind a wall of rocks and displayed an attitude even more sceptical than the governor's. But black and white was black and white, and Rowdy had had to accept the truth. He was a free man.

Whereupon he had succeeded in keeping himself as scarce as before; the months had passed and the press found other things to interest it. Rumour had Rowdy living in a remote mountain cabin and peacefully panning a little colour to keep himself in grub and tobacco. Rumour placed him in three different states at precisely the same time, and rumour, as usual, had a twisted tongue. For Rowdy, by long habit an ardent shunner of the limelight, had taken a *pasear* to Arizona in the company of a certain Stumpy Grampis, an uneventful trip that brought them back to Montana when Indian summer brushed its golden magic upon the land. And so Rowdy Dow came to Jubilee, that ungainly cowtown in the foothills of the Rockies, and came to the beginning of a great adventure. . . .

* * *

The awakening wasn't one to make a man relish the coming day. Rowdy stirred, groaned, and opened his eyes, but the darkness was so thick it could have been sliced, packaged, and sold for axle grease. The planking upon which he found himself bedded was hard as a lawman's heart, and his mouth tasted as though a family of squatters had just evacuated. Reaching out tentatively with his boot, Rowdy encountered company, and he said, "That you, Stumpy?"

Stumpy Grampis awoke with a litany of profanity that would have blistered paint. Rowdy, listening in appreciative awe, said, "We must have had ourselves a time last night."

"We had ourselves a time," Stumpy conceded. "We ripped off the lid and fastened 'er on crosswise. Where in blazes are we?"

"Back room of a saloon," Rowdy guessed. "I can smell drinking liquor. Only it's already been drunk. Maybe it's *you* I'm smelling."

"Likely," Stumpy agreed without rancour. "Say, we certainly roughed up that Bat Stull gent. Fancy runnin' into him in this—— Say, what in thunderation *is* the name of this town?"

"Bat Stull?" Rowdy said wonderingly. "Was he here?"

"It weren't his ghost."

"There must be easy money in this Jubilee country," Rowdy mused. "That big-bellied, loud-mouthed son calls himself an owlhooter, but he always plays a safe hand. So we run into him, eh?"

"We was likkerin' peaceable like, Rowdy. Must 'a' been our fourth or fifth saloon. Bat showed up outa nowhere and passed a few remarks about your gittin' a pardon. Hinted you must 'a' turned state's evidence again a few other fellers to have earned yourself that piece of paper. That was when you pulled his J. B. down over his eyes and kicked him in the chest."

"I let him off that easy?"

"I was on my hands and knees behind him when you made the play. Bat got his head wrapped up in a spittoon when he landed. Made quite a sight."

"Bat never rode alone in the old days," Rowdy recalled. "Wasn't his crew with him?"

"Seems there was four or five fellers. All of them was a

shade slow. I didn't throw more'n two bullets afore the bunch was clawin' at the ceiling and yowling for help.''

"I'm beginning to remember," Rowdy said. "It was the shooting that fetched the town marshal.''

Stumpy chuckled. "Do you recollect his face when we locked that tin-toter up in his own calaboose? But that's when the real trouble started. Danged if we could find the saloon when we headed back to it. Some sneakin' sons must 'a' moved it on us.''

"But we found another!'' Rowdy said, full recollection coming back to him. "And Federal Marshal Clee Drummond found us! Stumpy, this Jubilee was a mighty crowded town last night!''

"Drummond!'' Stumpy ejaculated. "That law dog was here, too? The last I recollected was the avalanche. It come a-roarin' down the mountain, sweepin' trees and boulders in front of it, and the whole mess come spillin' down on my head.''

"There wasn't any avalanche, Stumpy. Drummond pistol-whipped the pair of us. He laid his cutter between your horns, and then he must have did likewise to me.''

"I savvy!'' Stumpy roared. "We ain't in the back end of no saloon. *We're in the Jubilee calaboose!*''

"Let's have a look,'' Rowdy said.

They got to their feet, an effort that cost Rowdy a spinning sensation in the head, and they discovered a window in this tiny room that held them. They'd been squatting with their backs to the window, and it was now grey with the first light. Also, it was barred. Stumpy groaned aloud and said, "We're in the pokey all right. Drummond chased you a heap of miles when you was owlhootin', Rowdy. Likely he's laid for a chance like this. What do you reckon he'll do now?''

"We'll have to wait and see,'' said Rowdy Dow.

And that was the size of it. A pair of strangers, they had ridden into this town with a need for festivity in their restive souls. They had had themselves a time, and they had encountered two people they had known elsewhere. One had been Bat Stull, a man who skirted the ragged fringe of the law and made a dubious living without expending a great deal of the sweat of his brow. The other was Federal Marshal Clee Drummond, a relentless bloodhound of the law who was known from the Milk River to the Rio Grande.

They had bested the one and been bested by the other, and now they were in jail. The next card would be dealt by Clee Drummond.

The light grew stronger; it crept into the corners of the cell and revealed a crude cot, a washstand, a chair. Nothing more. They looked at each other and laughed, for they were both dirty and dishevelled, and they could have given a barber a busy hour. Rowdy wore bench-made boots, foxed trousers, and a pearl-buttoned shirt, and, in this garb, bore little resemblance to that one picture he'd had taken. He said, "Stumpy, dog-goned if the law won't give me thirty extra days in this hoosegow just for associating with a disreputable old hellion like you."

Stumpy Grampis was a little man, leathery and grizzled and with a sprinkling of frost in his thinning hair and down-tilted moustache. He had put more years behind him than he ever admitted; he had known the Montana of the open range, and he had seen the sodbuster come, bringing the plough and barbed wire and that perambulating pestilence, the tumbleweed. At times he'd turned his hand to toil; he'd been a freighter, a prospector, a cowhand, but mostly he'd seen the moon rise and listened to the owl hoot, as the saying went. Yet his description had never graced a reward dodger, a fact which didn't speak well for the efficiency of the law— and which rankled Stumpy no end. Nor had his picture ever appeared in the public prints. He had been with that festive group in Chinook the night Rowdy had been immortalised, but when the boys had lined up to pose, Stumpy had made the mistake of peeping under the black hood that draped the camera. To his utter horror, he had seen the entire group apparently standing on the ceiling. Whereupon Stumpy had broken his private bottle and collapsed in a corner, but not before taking a solemn vow that never so long as he lived would liquor again cross his alkali-cracked lips—a pledge which held in good effect for exactly eight hours.

His trail had again crossed with Rowdy Dow's after Rowdy had accepted the governor's pardon. Rowdy had been contemplating the Arizona trip, and the idea had likewise appealed to Stumpy, possessed always of an itchy foot. Stumpy had borrowed the pardon paper and scrawled his own name in with Rowdy's, thereby legally freeing himself, as far as he was concerned, from the interest of lawmen who had proved to be inconsiderately disinterested; and they had hit the trail. It was a circular trail, bringing them back to Montana. Most of Stumpy's life had been like that—filling out circles and ending up where he'd started.

Now Stumpy perked one hairy ear and said, "Listen, pard. Somebody's coming into the jail corridor."

It proved to be the town marshal they'd locked in this very jail the night before. A meek little man, he favoured them with a sour look as he paused before their cell door, and then he thrust a tray through an aperture designed for that purpose.

"Here's the breakfast," he said.

"Cawfee!" Stumpy chortled. "Pump the cream out of 'er and serve it black. That's my medicine."

"Hurry up with that grub," the town marshal said. "Clee Drummond wants to see you."

"Now you've soured the cream!" Stumpy groaned.

"Look, tin-badge," Rowdy said. "You haul your britches back to Clee Drummond and tell him we're indisposed this fine morning. If he's got an itch to palaver, he can come to *us*. Got that straight?"

The lawman made his departure with a flattering show of alacrity, and Stumpy, hoisting a fried egg on the end of a knife, said, "Drummond won't like that. No, sir!" But before he'd wiped the egg from his chin, boots were echoing along the corridor, and a high-shouldered figure came to a stop before the cell door. He said, "Howdy, boys. Mind if I just stand and look for a minute? Dow, I used to dream of seeing you on the inside of a set of bars."

"Howdy, Drummond," Rowdy said. "You certainly worked at it long enough."

Time had fashioned a legend out of Clee Drummond, though he didn't look the part. His garb would have suited a working cowhand, and his gun, walnut-handled, was nothing fancy; but it was the man himself who took the eye. He stood six feet high, and he stood as straight as a lodge-pole pine, though there was as much frost in his hair as there was in Stumpy Grampis's. His face was like granite covered with old parchment; sun and wind had dyed his skin to the colour of an Indian's. There was about him a wooden inscrutability that would have served at a poker table, and his eyes were heavy-lidded, giving an appearance of sleepiness. He smiled—a bleak movement of thin lips—and he said, "Yes, I worked hard at it. I spent a lot of time chasing you, Rowdy. But that was another day. I changed my mind about you when you made that ride down Calamity Valley three jumps ahead of a mountain of water."

"Don't believe all you read in the papers," Rowdy said. "I made that ride because I had to get out of the way of that busted dam. As far as the Paul Revere stuff was concerned, I was just shouting to keep myself awake. Some of the ranchers heard me and thought I was being a hero."

"And how do you like the quiet trails, Rowdy?"

Rowdy shrugged. "Was a time when I hankered to be a free man. Especially when I rode near a cowtown dance at night and heard the fiddles scraping and saw the young folks having fun. But I only learned one trade, Drummond. Nobody needs a man of my experience on the quiet trails."

"What brought you to Jubilee?"

"Heard that the railroad running through here was going to construct a spur to meet the main line on up north. Figured I might get a job toting the water bucket for the hard-working boys." He gestured impatiently. "Look, Drummond, I suppose I'm jugged for disturbing the peace. You can have the book thrown at me for, say, ninety days. Now run along and let me serve them. I don't have to answer your fool questions."

"I drifted in here yesterday afternoon," Drummond said. "The town marshal put me up. Professional courtesy, you might call it. You boys came, so I'm told, to have yourselves a fling. When you locked the town marshal up in this jail, his wife got me to let him out. I thought the pair of you ought to be cooled off before you busted something expensive. That's all. You're free to walk out as soon as you've finished breakfast."

Stumpy Grampis said, "There's somethin' goin' on behind them sleepy-looking eyes, Rowdy!!"

Drummond put his heavy-lidded gaze upon Stumpy. "I did have a piece of work in mind," he conceded.

"Then peddle it someplace else," Rowdy said. "I'm having no dealings with a law dog. Already, since I've hit this town, one smelly character has accused me of playing the law's game. Or maybe you don't know that Bat Stull and his bunch are around."

"I know," Drummond said. "In fact, they're trailing me."

"Trailing *you*——? That's hard to swallow!"

"I've turned in my badge," Drummond said. "Got a leave of absence from my work. To do a personal favour for a friend. Now I'm needing help. That's why I dragged you here, Rowdy. Sorry about that, but I had to sober you up so I could talk to you. You see, you and me are a pair of plain John Citizens this morning. But I can give you a chore that will make life as interesting as it ever was on the owlhoot. How about it?"

"Work that you were careful to shed your badge before tackling," Rowdy observed. "No dicker, mister! I don't want that pardon revoked."

"So you'll do no favour for me," Drummond said. "But will you do a favour for Butch Rafferty? Or aren't you old enough for that name to have any meaning to you?"

"Rafferty!" Rowdy ejaculated, and his eyes lighted. "Do you think there's a man in Montana who never heard of Butch Rafferty and his Wild Bunch? But Butch has been in Deer Lodge pen for nearly ten years, and his old gang is dead or scattered to the Argentine. What kind of a windy is this?"

"Less than two months ago I sat in the prison hospital in Deer Lodge and talked to Butch Rafferty," Drummond said. "He told me where I could lay my hands on a certain article. It took a long ride to reach the place where Rafferty had left that article—an old shack in the Jackson Hole country, down in Wyoming. But I found it."

Rowdy's interest had quickened, but he hid his curiosity behind a quick fumbling for the makings, and he shaped up a cigarette before he said, "Go on."

"About an hour from now, a train pulls through Jubilee to climb over the hump of the hills and drop down into Latigo Basin. I want you on that train, Rowdy. You'll take the article to John Crenshaw's ranch in Latigo Basin. I'll meet you there and you'll turn the article over to me. If I should fail to show up in, say, a week, you'll surrender it to John Crenshaw. Are you interested?"

"Why don't you tote it yourself?"

"Because Bat Stull knows I've got it, and Stull is going to make a play to take it away from me, either here in

Jubilee, or somewhere before I reach Latigo. This is my way of fooling Stull. He'll never suspect that I've turned it over to you.''

''Must be pretty valuable, that doojigger, to tempt Stull into sticking his neck out that far,'' Rowdy decided.

''When we meet at Crenshaw's ranch, I'll tell you how valuable it is,'' Drummond said. ''Until then, you'll have to take my word that it's absolutely necessary that you get it through.''

''What's in it for me?''

''A cash pay-off when you deliver. Possibly a thousand dollars. Take it or leave it. I said you could walk out of here anytime. But I *could* whisper a word to the town marshal and he *might* throw the book at you for ninety days. He doesn't like you boys. You play too rough.''

''We'd better do his fetching for him, Rowdy,'' Stumpy said sourly. ''He's ornery enough to keep us cooling here.''

There was this about Rowdy Dow; he made his decisions fast. He said, ''I'll be on that train, Drummond. First, because it happens that I owe Butch Rafferty a favour, and I'm taking your word that delivering the article will please Rafferty. Second, because I don't crave to sit in this pokey another night. And third, because tangling Bat Stull's twine is a nice way of passing the time. Now let's have this article that's so valuable it's got both you and Stull into a lather.''

''Here it is,'' said Clee Drummond. Extending his closed fist between the bars, he dropped into Rowdy's palm a tiny china figurine, so small that it could be held hidden in a man's hand—a figurine moulded into the shape of a rearing stallion.

2. Bat Stull

To ROWDY, emerging from the jail building with Stumpy Grampis, Jubilee had that morning-after-the-night-before look, and he regarded the town sourly before starting along the rickety boardwalk. Even to a less jaundiced eye, Jubilee would have hardly qualified as a thing of beauty and a joy forever. Its main street was erratic and dusty, and obviously a single-minded architect had designed the buildings, for there was a preponderance of plain siding and false fronts. Some of the buildings were spaced apart, with weed-choked, debris-littered lots between them. But some shouldered each other so closely that local legend had it that a man given to tossing in his sleep might bed down in the Mountain View Hotel and awake in the morning to find himself in Nels Borgreen's blacksmith shop, five doors away. Stumpy, who'd found this a town of sad experience, was inclined to believe.

"We rented us a hotel room when we first come," Stumpy recalled. "Now I suppose they've moved the dang hotel, same as they did that saloon. I tell you, there's dishonesty rampant hereabouts."

Rowdy said nothing. He had gotten the feeling that eyes were upon him, but the instincts of the owlhoot kept him from betraying this fact. There were few people on the street—a shopkeeper or two sweeping off the boardwalks before their establishments, a whiskered individual snoozing peacefully beneath a saloon's wooden awning. But many windows looked upon them, and the warning persisted within Rowdy. When the two came abreast of a livery stable, Rowdy abruptly turned inside, his quick nudge directing Stumpy to do likewise.

10

The hostler had sleep in his eyes and hay in his hair. To him Rowdy said, "We left a couple of cayuses here yesterday afternoon for graining and rest."

"They got both," the hostler reported. "You taking those jugheads?"

"Mind your language!" Rowdy admonished him. "Those horses have been ridden by crowned heads. Fact is, they're so sensitive that we ride 'em one week, and then we have to let them ride the next week. That being the case, will you load them into the first stock car going over the hump into Latigo?"

"The passenger train comes through to-day," the hostler explained. "The freight will likely be along to-morrow."

Stumpy became inspired. "Trains bother my asthma, Rowdy. Mebbe so, we could fork our critters over the hump."

Rowdy got the drift. If Marshal Clee Drummond wanted them to transport that toy stallion so that Bat Stull, not suspecting, would continue to think that Drummond had the figurine, perhaps it might even be wiser to alter Drummond's plan and travel by horseback. Thus if there were any leaks in the plans Stull would again be fooled. Glancing at the hostler, Rowdy said, "What about that, feller? How's horseback travel over the hump?"

The owner of this fragrant establishment shook his head. "For the first few hours you could make even better time than the train. The railroad swings miles south to avoid a steep ridge, then turns north, practically makin' a horseshoe. Cayuses can hump over that ridge, but most of the time you'd be afoot and leading them. But when the real climbing comes, over Latigo Pass and down into the basin, the train's got the edge. Horses can make that pass, but only providing that one of their grandpappys was a mountain goat."

"We'll ship the horses," Rowdy decided and produced money. "And now show us the back door. I never go out the same way I come in. Fellow sees more scenery that way."

The hostler let them into an alley, and Rowdy hurried the bewildered Stumpy to a faster gait. "There's only one hotel in town," Rowdy said. "I spotted it from the street. We'll go in the back way. Somebody's been watching us ever since we stepped out of the jail, old-timer. Let 'em figure we're still in the livery stable.''

"I'm beginning to think this whole business is loco," Stumpy grumbled. "Clee Drummond is making a couple of clowns outa us, just to tickle his own private sense o' humour. Who in tarnation would want that little hoss?''

"Drummond shoved a wad of expense money into my paw just before we left the jail," Rowdy countered. "He's entitled to laugh till that money runs out. Nope, there's more here than meets the eye, old son. Say, isn't this the hotel?''

They came in through the back door of one of the few Jubilee establishments that boasted two storeys, and they threaded their way to a small lobby littered with horsehair chairs and sofas and some sickly-looking imitation palms. An aged clerk dozed behind a desk, and two men hunkered deep in the chairs, but both had newspapers spread open before their faces and were busily reading, so Rowdy was certain he was unobserved as he quietly edged Stumpy up the carpeted stairs. Stumpy said, "We need a key to our room.''

"Got a skeleton in my pocket," Rowdy said. "Should have mailed it to the governor, I reckon, after he sent me that pardon, just as a sign of good faith. But I never got around to it.''

The upper hallway was comfortingly empty. They held a whispered argument about the number of their room, Rowdy contending that it was six, while Stumpy insisted that it was nine, and when it developed that there were only eight rooms in the establishment, Rowdy smiled his triumph. He fumbled with the skeleton only to find that the door gave beneath his hand. It was then he realised that something was almighty wrong, but it was too late.

The room within was nothing to gladden a wayfarer's heart. There was a faded carpet, a rickety bed, a teetering bureau, and a washstand that had obviously been made from a discarded packing case. And seated upon the bed in such a position as to face the door when it opened was Bat Stull, a gun in his hand. He was a big man, this Stull, broad of shoulders and broad of face and with an expanse of stomach that sagged over his gunbelt. Yet there was a lot of strength in that immense carcass, and a lot of devilry, too. It showed in his swarthy face, and in his small, piggish eyes.

Stull said jovially, "Come in, boys! Come in. That's right. With your hands up. Jackson, relieve them of their guns and drop them in the corner."

The man who stepped from behind the opened door was a giant. There was over six feet of him, and he must have tallied better than two hundred pounds, and none of it was excess baggage. A worn sombrero was shoved back to reveal a closely-shaven skull which might have interested an anthropologist. There was a lot of head there, but very little brain. The eyes were vacuous, and with Rowdy and Stumpy ranged along the wall, Jackson stolidly went about the business of unlatching their gun-belts and tossing them to a far corner.

"Now," said Bat Stull, "we can talk. You boys haven't met Jackson. Stonehead Jackson, they call him. Late of Deer Lodge pen. A remarkable critter, Jackson. You've maybe read in the papers about Blind Tom, the nigger piano player who's been in vaudeville for quite a few years. Blind Tom's a simple fellow with no musical training, but they say that that black boy can play any old tune after hearing it once. Stonehead, here, is talented in a slightly different way. Reel off any kind of speech to him, and he can repeat it afterwards. The speech may not make any sense to him, but he gets 'er down to the last comma. You wouldn't believe it, would you?"

"No," said Rowdy, "I wouldn't believe it."

Stull grinned. "Listen, Jackson," he ordered. " 'Four score and seven years ago . . .' "

" 'Four score and seven years ago our fathers brought forth upon this continent,' " Jackson intoned, " 'a new nation, conceived in liberty . . .' " Whereupon he recited all of Lincoln's Gettysburg Address, his voice flat and lifeless, but never faltering, never missing a word. Rowdy was impressed, and Stumpy even more so. "A danged parrot, that's what the man is!" Stumpy ejaculated.

Rowdy said, "That's mighty interesting, Bat. But you didn't come up here to put on a free show. How did you get into the room, and what do you want?"

But he knew what Stull wanted, or at least he thought he did. This was what Rowdy had feared, a leak in Clee Drummond's plans, and that meant that Stull was here to take that china stallion from him. Or was he? Maybe Stull, remembering the indignity of the night before when Rowdy had booted him over the appropriately placed form of Stumpy Grampis, had come to exact revenge and was having himself a time with a cat-and-mouse prelude. In either case, Rowdy cursed his own carelessness. He'd taken precautions in getting out of the livery stable and into the hotel, but Bat Stull had anticipated him.

"How did I get in?" Stull laughed, a full-bodied boisterous laugh that Rowdy had always found irritating. "Talked the clerk out of your key. Told him we was old friends from up Chinook way and that I wanted to surprise you. The last was no lie."

Then, amazingly, Stull cased his gun. "Lower your paws, boys. I'm not sore. Last night is water under the bridge. We all had a little too much fightin' whisky in us."

"A most loving and forgiving town," Rowdy said. "Everybody is just crazy to kiss and make up."

"Meaning Clee Drummond?" Stull asked quickly. "He loaded you boys into jail last night. Now you're out."

"He had no authority," Rowdy said. "He was just repping for the town marshal. The local tin-toter could have kept us for disturbing the peace, but he decided that he might have to rebuild his pokey afterwards if he did. That's all there was to it."

He was watching Stull closely, and he knew that if Stull didn't challenge his story, then Stull had no inkling that the china stallion was at that very moment in Rowdy's possession.

"We had an eye on the jail," Stull said. "Sooner or later you was bound to come out. Likewise we knew that you'd taken this hotel room. Found your name on the register. You had to pick up your war-sack before leaving. It was just a matter of waiting. Rowdy, you don't like me, and I ain't loco about you. But I've got a job to do where you'd be a help. Mister, I'm here to cut you in on one hundred thousand easy dollars in good old gold money!"

The war-sack referred to lay on the floor at the end of the bed. Rowdy crossed to it and began fumbling with the draw string, an act that instantly brought Stull's gun back into his hand and even caused the silent Stonehead Jackson, who stood with arms folded, to start nervously. Rowdy said, "Keep your shirts nailed down, boys. I'm not after a hideout gun. I'm looking for my shaving gear. I've heard these easy money stories before. They always turn out to be wasted time. But if I get the whiskers off my face while I'm listening, then I can't lose.''

Fumbling for his razor and brush, he found them, and he stripped off his shirt and tested the water in the pitcher on the washstand with an experimental finger. He handed the pitcher to Stonehead Jackson. ''Run downstairs and see if you can talk the desk clerk out of some hot water,'' he said.

Jackson turned his gaze upon Bat Stull, who nodded. When the giant was gone, Stull said, ''It's best not to talk in front of him. Might start that midget brain of his to working, and he'd likely spiel off the *whole* story. You see, Jackson was just let out of Deer Lodge pen a month ago. Served a few years for horse stealing. Before they turned him loose, they put him in the prison hospital for observation— the question being whether to free him or transfer him to the institution with the padded walls.''

''Sure,'' said Rowdy. ''And under the hospital bed he found one hundred thousand bucks in gold.''

''Nope, but in the next bed was Butch Rafferty.''

Rowdy's interest quickened, but he didn't show it. ''And Rafferty spun him a windy about loot he'd buried back in the days when the Wild Bunch was making a name for themselves?''

''Now you're getting warm,'' Stull said. ''You acquainted in Latigo Basin?''

''Never been near it,'' Rowdy said truthfully.

''Neither have me or my boys. There's a rancher over that way who likewise has been running the Latigo bank for a long time. Name's John Crenshaw. Well, it seems that Butch Rafferty, years ago, stuck up a stagecoach that was hauling one hundred thousand dollars in gold to John Crenshaw's bank. Clee Drummond came to call on Butch Rafferty in the prison hospital while Jackson was in the next bed. Seems that Drummond wanted to find out what had become of that hundred thousand, and, since Rafferty's combined sentences add up to more than life imprisonment, and, since Rafferty's bunch is dead or gone, Drummond figgered that Rafferty might tell where that money was hid, once some circumstances were explained. Them circumstances don't matter. The point is that——''

The door opened, and Stonehead Jackson appeared with a steaming pitcher. When Rowdy had taken it, Stull said, "Step out in the hall and keep an eye on things, Jackson." The giant silently obeyed.

All this while, Rowdy Dow had been thinking of many things. He was greatly interested in Bat Stull's story—it filled in some gaps in what Clee Drummond had had to say—but mostly Rowdy was concerned about the passing minutes. Drummond had mentioned that the train would be passing through Jubilee in about an hour. Rowdy had to be on that train. Working lather out of a bar of soap, he covered his beard. Stull said wonderingly, "Do you always keep your hat on while you're shaving?

"I don't shave the *top* of my head," Rowdy said. "Now were you going to tell me that Butch Rafferty was crazy enough to tell Clee Drummond where he could lay his hands on that money?"

"Once Drummond had done some talking, Rafferty was," Stull said. "Jackson joined up with me after he got out. At first I figured the big galoot wouldn't be worth taking along. But one night he got reciting the whole conversation he'd overheard. Yes, Rafferty was willing to string along. Only Rafferty didn't know where the money had been hidden."

Rowdy shrugged. "You see, I was smart in spending this time at shaving." And he began scraping away with the razor.

"Butch Rafferty was a Robin Hood sort of galoot," Stull said. "He made friends, and those friends helped him. There was a string of ranches stretching from the Canadian to the Mexican border where Rafferty's bunch could get themselves fresh horses and a bite of grub and no questions asked. Everybody knows that, now. One of those ranches was in Latigo Basin."

"You always keep coming back to Latigo Basin, Stull."

"And for a reason. That's where Rafferty stopped the stage and got John Crenshaw's money. And that's where Rafferty left it—at a ranch. A posse was crowding him, and Rafferty was short of time, and that gold made considerable weight. So he turned it over to his rancher friend with orders for the man to hide it. And then Rafferty grabbed something off a shelf in that ranch-house. A little hoss made out of chinaware. And he told the rancher that if he, Rafferty, didn't come back for the dinero, he'd send somebody else—maybe in a month, maybe in a year, maybe in ten years. Whoever came for the money would show that china stallion. And friend rancher swore he'd surrender it to the man with the toy hoss.''

"Sure," said Rowdy, rinsing the lather from his face. "And as soon as that rancher gent heard that Rafferty was gone to Deer Lodge for the rest of his life, the rancher dug up the dinero and had himself a spree spending it."

"No man would double-cross Butch Rafferty while Rafferty was still alive. Not even with Rafferty in stony lonesome. Rafferty's convinced that the money's still around. So's Drummond. Convinced enough that he sashayed down to the Jackson Hole country to an old Rafferty hideout and got that china stallion. But meanwhile we'd got the story out of Jackson and taken Drummond's trail. He's here in Jubilee now—one jump from Latigo Basin. But a couple of my boys are watching that jail building. When he shows himself and starts for the livery stable, I'll know it. We'll be the ones to head for Latigo Basin with the china stallion."

Rowdy wiped his razor and put it away, then lifted his head at the sound of a train whistle. One long blast. That meant a mile sign out of Jubilee. "And you want to cut me in on this?" Rowdy asked.

"It's big, Rowdy. Bigger than anything I've ever tackled. And it's Clee Drummond we're bucking. I've got good boys, feller, but they're not long on the think. This is a job of your calibre, only I was afraid to trust you until you got so damned resentful of being accused of siding the law last night. We split even all around."

"And who's the rancher in Latigo that's going to turn over that dinero when somebody puts a china stallion in his hand?"

Stull grinned broadly. "And once you know that, you can make the play lone-handed. No deal, Rowdy. Not unless you throw in with us."

Rowdy shrugged into his shirt. "It's no deal anyway," he said. "I've got a pardon. I'm anxious to keep it. That hundred thousand is going to be hotter than Satan's private tea pot. So you'll have to get somebody else to do the dirtier side of the work. That was your idea, wasn't it? I'd take the risks, and you'd collect the dinero?"

The show of joviality faded from Stull's little eyes. "I was counting on you, Rowdy," he said slowly. "Counting a heap." He reached for the gun at his hip. "But you won't come in, and that means I can't let you leave here alive. I've told you too much for that. Don't look toward that door. Stonehead Jackson's out in the hall, and two of my other boys are sitting down in the lobby. Maybe you saw 'em. And there's another outside, keeping his eye peeled for you."

Again the train whistle sounded, this time much closer. Two long blasts, a short and a long one. That meant it was signalling for the road crossing just before it reached Jubilee's depot. And Rowdy, moving quickly, grasped the basin of soapy, lukewarm water he'd used in shaving and hurled its contents full into Bat Stull's swarthy face.

3. The Backward Track

THE TRAIN THAT TWINED through the hills and into Jubilee this day consisted of a locomotive which reluctantly towed a baggage car and a day coach behind it. This locomotive possessed an erratic and diabolical personality; it chuffed and snorted across the miles, making a great clatter and a great show of speed while it smeared a broad banner of smoke against the sky, yet, in spite of this, it always contrived to arrive at least fashionably late at every station. It was a most discontented locomotive. It had been promised retirement, a full ten years before, but office politics was keeping it in harness. Therefore the train crew, a distraught group of men, swore that the locomotive was exacting revenge by being deliberately perverse.

They reiterated this weird contention in Jubilee. For here the engine came to a stop and waited docilely while mail and baggage were unloaded and while the conductor ascertained that no prospective passengers were at the depot, but when the time came to be moving again, the locomotive refused to budge. Absolutely. Threats and blandishments failed, the train crew held frantic consultations, and the engineer lifted his clenched fists to the unsympathetic heavens and demanded to know by what justice such a curse as this had been placed upon him in his declining years. Exactly nothing happened.

Two of the passengers, made curious by the long wait, clambered down from the day coach. One, a well-knit man in his mid-twenties with a good-looking face that was given to smiling, took a professional interest in the delay. He was Logan MacLean, employed by the railroad in a high capacity, and en route to Latigo on business known only to himself and his superiors. Young MacLean had heard the legend of the discontented locomotive, and, though he was a man of imagination, his fancy didn't stretch that far. He had a look at the situation and offered some advice which put new hope in the engineer.

The second passenger, meanwhile, was contenting himself with standing on the depot platform, his eyes lifted to the high hills that stood between Jubilee and Latigo Basin. He was a man to take the eye, for he was tall and slender and bare-headed, his thick brown hair brushed back from a classic brow. His suit was dark and well-tailored, and he wore a long cape which gave him an Old World air and a touch of mystery. His graven face was unreadable. A patient man, this one, used to delays along whatever path he followed . . .

All this while, those two potential passengers for the temperamental train, Rowdy Dow and Stumpy Grampis, were keeping themselves exceedingly busy . . .

As Rowdy hurled the soapy water into Bat Stull's face, he followed this act by throwing himself upon the big man while Stull was frantically pawing at his eyes and trying to get his gun unleathered at the same time. Rowdy got his fingers around the wrist of Stull's gun-hand, and he brought his free fist against Stull's blocky jaw in a chopping blow. The bed collapsed beneath their combined weights, and from the hallway came a wild rumble of sound, proof enough that Stonehead Jackson realised that something was almighty wrong.

But Stumpy Grampis was into action, too. Stull, after talking the desk clerk out of the key and admitting himself to this room, had adroitly transferred the key to the inside keyhole so that Rowdy, approaching the door, had not realised there was anything amiss. A bound took Stumpy to the door, and he twisted the key. Outside, Jackson roared: "Bat! What you doing in there?"

"If that big blockhead throws those shoulders of his'n agin that door, he'll likely tear out this side of the building!" Stumpy gasped, but Rowdy was too busy to hear him. Rowdy was exerting all his effort in keeping Stull from reaching that gun, and Stumpy, seeing his partner's intent, succeeded in plucking the gun away from the writhing Stull and hurling it aside. Then Stumpy, inspired, grabbed his own gun from the corner, his intent to lay the barrel across Stull's head. But Stull had gone limp beneath Rowdy and lay back upon the debris of the bed.

"A glass jaw," Rowdy panted. "The jigger had a glass jaw."

Stonehead Jackson was rattling the doorknob so violently that a sun-faded and obsolete calendar, hanging upon the wall, jiggled madly. "Quit that, you big ox!" Rowdy roared authoritatively. "Get down to the lobby and fetch the boys up here. Poor Bat has had a fainting spell!"

He held his breath, not knowing whether Jackson would become more infuriated by this piece of news or would automatically obey. There was hesitation out in the hall, manifested by an abrupt silence, and Rowdy tried to visualise the workings of that freakish brain. Then Jackson's boots were beating a thunderous tattoo as the giant hurried toward the stairs.

"You're loosin' yore grip, Rowdy," Stumpy complained. "What do you figger to gain by gettin' Stull's men upstairs?"

Rowdy was picking up his gun-belt and buckling it on, and he dug frantically into his war-sack. "Got a spare lariat packed," he said, and withdrew the rope. Quickly tying an end around the doorknob, Rowdy played out the rope across the room and, heaving up the sash, tossed the coil from the window. "Out you go," he ordered Stumpy.

Stumpy obeyed with alacrity, and when the little oldster had passed himself hand over hand down to the ground, Rowdy tossed the war-sack down to him. Then Rowdy was clambering over the sill, but boots were thundering in the hall again, many of them, and the knob was being rattled. Bat Stull's name was called by two different voices, and someone shouted, "Bust the door down, Jackson! Bust it down!"

Rowdy burned his hands on the rope, making a much faster descent than Stumpy had, and midway the rope jerked violently, and Rowdy, feeling himself drop a full yard, knew that the door had burst inward. He let go then, landing cat-like on the ground at the side of the building, and he and Stumpy were instantly heading for the rear of the hotel, the war-sack dangling between them.

"Forgot to pay our room rent!" Stumpy panted.

"Let 'em collect from Stull," Rowdy said. "My dear old friend from Chinook!"

Heads bobbed out of the upper storey window they'd just quitted—two of them—and Rowdy, looking back, caught the flash of early morning sunlight upon gun-barrels. Whereupon the peace of Jubilee was completely shattered by the roar of six-shooters. But Rowdy and his partner were rounding the corner to what might have been comparative safety except that a man loomed before them, a tall, stringy, unshaven man, bent upon obvious business.

Bat Stull had mentioned that one of his crew had been posted outside as insurance against Rowdy's departure from the Mountain View Hotel without the presence, and thereby the blessing, of Stull. This was very definitely the man. Rowdy had seen the fellow in Stull's company in the past, and recognition was mutual.

Surprise gave Rowdy and his partner the advantage. And Stumpy utilised it in a manner most efficient. Without breaking his stride the little oldster lowered his head and ploughed into Stull's man, catching the fellow full in the midriff. The man went down, clutching his stomach and with the breath whooshing out of him, and Rowdy and Stumpy rounded another corner and headed for the street.

This strategy had been Rowdy's and was designed to send Stull's men seeking the alleyways for their quarry—a search that was bound to be futile. In the street, Rowdy made for the depot at a hard run, for the train was chuffing energetically. The magic of Logan MacLean had worked, and it was going to be touch and go to make it to the far end of the street where the depot squatted. And Rowdy groaned as he risked another backward look, for men were spilling from the front of the Mountain View—three of them—and the bigness of Stonehead Jackson was unmistakable.

These men still had guns in their hands, and they spied the fleeing two and began peppering the bullets about them, and that gave Rowdy the devil's own choice. If he sought the shelter of the buildings that flanked them on either side and made a fight, he'd miss the train. But if he concentrated on getting to the depot by the most direct route, he'd have to stay out here in the open street, an easy target for those men before the hotel. He tugged at his own gun, intending to compromise by scattering a little lead, and when he turned to aim he saw the three scurrying back into the hotel.

At first that didn't make sense, and then Rowdy realised that someone else had taken cards in this game. Farther up the street, beyond the hotel, a man stood spread-legged on the steps before the jail, a smoking six-shooter in his hand; and that had been the persuasion that had diverted Stull's men from their original intent.

Rowdy said, "Clee Drummond! First time I ever wanted to kiss a badge-toter!"

Facing forward again, he put everything into the task of reaching the depot. Stumpy was panting loudly, sounding not a little like a ruptured accordion, and the train was moving as the pair rounded the depot and charged across the platform. The conductor was just closing the rear door to the day coach, but he saw them coming and held it open. With a mighty heave, Rowdy sent the war-sack sailing, almost bowling over the conductor, and then Rowdy had swung aboard and was dragging Stumpy into the coach's vestibule.

"You boys running away from a lynch mob?" the conductor demanded.

Rowdy pressed money into the man's hand. "Just winning a bet, Skipper. We claimed we could give this cast-iron cayuse a running start and reach it from any part of town."

"I heard shooting," the conductor said darkly.

"The boys who had their money on us were celebrating," Rowdy explained. "They knew it was a cinch."

He shouldered on into the coach, Stumpy trailing after him. There were only five other passengers. One was young Logan MacLean, seated toward the rear; another was the still-faced man in the cape who gave the newcomers a casual glance and then resumed gazing from the window. A fat tobacco drummer sprawled almost the width of a seat, and, across from Logan MacLean sat a blue-eyed, sweet-faced girl beside a silent creature in the long black dress and veil of a widow.

Rowdy took the seat behind these two, whom he judged to be mother and daughter, and Stumpy slid in beside him. Jubilee was falling behind, the train gathered momentum, and Rowdy breathed an expansive sigh of relief. "Danged if I ain't gonna retire in another ten years or so," Stumpy grumbled. "Gittin' too old for this kind of fool nonsense."

Rowdy was contemplating the neck of the girl ahead of them. It was a nice neck, sculptured along the proper lines and with a neat bun of brown hair resting upon it. The trip promised to be long and monotonous, and he considered attempting her acquaintance, but he remembered a parting injunction of Clee Drummond's. "I don't need to tell you to keep your mouth shut about this chore," the marshal had said. "But above all, watch yourself while you're on the train. You can just about figure that anybody you'll find aboard will be headed for Latigo-town. So don't go wagging your tongue at them."

Which, Rowdy reflected, showed you how some men's minds worked. Now who'd go bothering that pretty girl with a lot of crazy palaver about a little china horse that now seemed to be the key to one hundred thousand hidden dollars? Or telling her of the necessity to deliver that horse to the ranch of a certain John Crenshaw? A travelled man, and one lately in the public eye, Rowdy could ease the boredom of her journey with accounts of far places and momentous events. He tapped her lightly on the shoulder and said, experimentally, "Would you or your mother mind if I smoked, Miss?"

The girl turned her head, and the profile would have done grace to a Grecian coin. But her voice was cold enough to have been made out of the same ancient metal. "I'm sure it doesn't matter," she said. "Please don't disturb us. Can't you see that my mother has just recently been bereaved?"

"Sorry, Miss," Rowdy said sincerely and forgot about the makings—both Virginia-grown and conversational.

He left her alone after that; he had an instinctive gallantry in such matters, and he amused himself by studying the other passengers. Logan MacLean had fished some sort of manual from a pocket of the grey suit he wore and was busily scanning the pages, but Rowdy soon detected that the young man often stole covert glances at the girl across the aisle. Rowdy wondered if that young bucko had tried making himself acquainted, too, and just how soundly he'd gotten set back upon his ear.

The man in the cape held Rowdy's interest for a while, but that man, by his very manner, was keeping himself thoroughly isolated from all others, and Rowdy drew his eyes away. Yet the man was not so easily dismissed from mind. There was something about him that stayed with Rowdy, some suggestion of power and of a driving purpose that defied analysis.

The miles unreeled monotonously, a blur of timber flashed past on either side of the track, and sometimes the train hooted dismally at it. The frowning hills seemed to be getting no nearer, in fact the train appeared to be skirting them, and the grade remained level. An hour passed and another, and Rowdy became acutely aware that it had been a long time since breakfast. The train rounded a hairpin turn, but nothing changed. There was still that same vista of screening timber and hills that got no closer.

"Say!" Stumpy suddenly announced. "Ever since we left Jubilee we've been going straight south. Now we're heading due north. You reckon we're going to end up back in Jubilee?"

"Don't you remember?" Rowdy said. "The livery stable man explained how the tracks skirt a ridge and then cut around it and come back before climbing the mountains."

"A helluva way to run a railroad!" Stumpy grumbled.

Rowdy hunkered down in the seat, carefully eased his sombrero over his nose and dozed for a while, hoping to forget his hunger, but it seemed that he'd no sooner gotten asleep when the train shuddered to a bone-jarring stop. Rowdy's quick glance from the window showed him the same expanse of crowding timber, and Stumpy said complacently, "Water tank here."

The girl ahead was busily straightening the wide hat and veil of her companion which had apparently been jarred by the sudden stop. Rowdy righted his own headgear, stretched luxuriously and then suddenly stiffened as his eye caught a quick movement beyond the window. A man was stalking beside the stopped coach, bending low and trying to keep from view of the passengers inside. And that man was Stonehead Jackson.

Understanding came quickly to Rowdy, for the Jubilee hostler had told him that riders could climb the ridge and reach this farther track ahead of the train. And riders had done just exactly that—riders headed by Bat Stull. Rowdy reached for his gun then, but he never touched it, for a blocky form had appeared at the far end of the coach, and the wavering gun in the man's hand covered every passenger.

"Take it easy, folks," the blocky man advised. "There'll be no harm done any of you. This ain't a real stick-up. There's just one thing we're after."

Bat Stull had a bandanna up over his nose, but there was no mistaking the man. He came a few steps farther into the car, and other masked men crowded at his heels. With these to keep surveillance over the rest of the passengers, Stull advanced upon Rowdy. The girl ahead gasped quickly, making no other sound than that; Logan MacLean had stiffened, and even the man in the cloak had been shaken from his imperturbability to an alert interest. But to these Bat Stull paid not the slightest heed.

"Fork it over, Rowdy," he said.

"Fork what over?"

Stull laughed his booming, irritating laugh. "You fooled me slicker'n calf slobber, Rowdy," he said. "But after the train pulled out, Clee Drummond went to the livery stable for his horse. We cornered him there, and he didn't have the china stallion, and he wouldn't tell us what had become of it. But we began putting two and two together. Drummond was in the jail when you were there this morning. And later Drummond sided you when you made that run for the train."

"And you think I've got that toy horse?"

"Who else?" Stull countered, and the joviality went out of his voice. "Now are you gonna fork it over, or do we have to peel you down to the skin and find it for ourselves?"

4. Who's Got the Horse?

ONE OF STULL'S MEN, stepping around Bat, quickly relieved Rowdy and Stumpy of their guns, and, since this was the second time in a single day that Rowdy had been so deprived by this particular group, he reflected that the procedure was growing mighty monotonous. Also, he reflected that some fast thinking was very much in order. But Logan MacLean suddenly bought into the affair, coming to a high stand and looking as though he'd forgotten to count ten before letting go on his temper.

"You fellows can't get away with this!" MacLean snapped. "I work for the railroad, and I'll see you all in jail for this outrage. Unless you put up those guns and pile off this train."

Another of Stull's men placed the flat of his hand against MacLean's chest and shoved hard. "Sit down!" the fellow said, unnecessarily. "This ain't your affair."

There was enough fight in MacLean that anything could happen now, and Rowdy's instant decision was that that young man needed to be saved from the consequences of an injudicious wrath. So Rowdy grinned widely. "You're holding the aces, Stull," he conceded. "But how about a deal? I'm as hungry as a woodpecker with a busted beak. Lead me to a campfire with a coffee pot bubbling over it, and I'll tell you how you can get hold of that china horse."

Stull nearly strangled. "A deal——!" he spluttered. "We don't have to dicker. Don't you savvy? We're here to take that hoss away from you!"

"Look," Rowdy said wearily. "I haven't got the horse. Search me and you'll find that out. But you're right about me stringing along with Clee Drummond."

The train whistle spoke impatiently, the cars trembled to the master's touch, and these symptoms of departure spurred Stull to a decision. "Pile off!" he ordered. "Both of you. And fetch that war-sack along. We'll *see* who's got the china stallion."

Rowdy shrugged, came to a stand, politely let Stumpy pass him and proceed up the aisle, but as Rowdy came abreast of the girl's seat, he paused, swung to face her, doffed his sombrero and made a sweeping bow. "My apologies," he said solemnly. "I hope this disturbance hasn't caused you or your mother any great trouble."

Stull's gun-barrel prodded Rowdy's spine. "Never mind that," Stull urged. "Get off before the train pulls out."

They came up the aisle to the vestibule, captors and captives, leaving a deathly silence behind them. The conductor was crowded against a wall, his hands high and a gun pressed against the third brass button on his coat. In passing, Rowdy gave the man a broad wink and said, "So long, Skipper. Remember that me and my pard have a rebate to collect on our train fare. Haven't used up more than a third of it."

The train was moving as the last man alighted. Rowdy got a glimpse of Logan MacLean's face as the coach slid by, and he grinned at that very earnest young man's show of anger and dismay. Stull's crew was busy at fetching horses from the timber, and, although seven men had ridden here, there were nine mounts—proof that Stull had foreseen just such an exigency as this. Rowdy and his partner were urged up into saddles, and, with the group bunched around them, they went riding off into the screening timber.

Stull said, "That young railroad feller meant business. We'd better put the tracks considerable behind us."

Stumpy broke what had been an unusually long silence for him. "When we eatin'?" he demanded.

They were following a game trail that paralleled the railroad track and began climbing steadily upward, and where the timber thinned to make a sort of meadow, Stull suddenly hauled on his reins. "It's come to me," he said, "that Dow might be bluffing. Down, everybody. We're going over him with a fine-tooth comb."

And they did. The war-sack was turned inside out and its contents examined minutely. Both Rowdy and Stumpy were forced to strip, a none-too-pleasant experience at this time of year and at this altitude, and every garment was passed from hand to hand. All of which netted exactly nothing of real interest to Stull and his men, and anger was written on every face except the bland and vacuous one that belonged to Stonehead Jackson. As Rowdy and his partner dressed, Stull said coldly, "Where is it, Dow?"

"You've forgotten the bargain," Rowdy replied. "Something to eat, first."

Stull's broad face purpled. "There wasn't any bargain. If I build a fire, it will be to burn the soles of your feet. Maybe that will get the truth out of you!"

Rowdy sighed. "Now what do you figure to gain by being so confounded stubborn?"

Stull's shoulders sagged in resignation. "Start a fire, boys," he said. "And fish out the coffee pan and skillet. We'll try killin' this galoot with kindness."

It was obvious that some of Stull's men would have preferred other methods. The tall, stringy one whom Stumpy Grampis had met head-on behind the Mountain View Hotel in Jubilee had been scowling ever since they'd left the train. But they obeyed Stull; food and cooking utensils were fetched from saddle bags and a fire was quickly built, and soon the coffee was bubbling and bacon was curling up contentedly in a frying pan. When the tin plates were passed and emptied, Stull said, "Well——?"

Rowdy sighed. Between sips from a steaming cup, he said, "Well, sir, you could have knocked me down with a wagon tongue when Clee Drummond fetched me a proposition in the Jubilee jail early this morning. Seems he'd gotten hold of a little china horse, and he was mighty anxious to get that horse to Latigo Basin. But you boys were sticking to him tighter than his skin."

"So he gave you the horse?" Stull demanded eagerly.

Rowdy took another sip. "Mighty good coffee," he decided. "You could float a horseshoe in it, and I always say——"

"The horse!" Stull thundered.

"Oh, yeah, the horse. Well, sir, Clee Drummond had an idea. He figured to stay in Jubilee and let me go on to Latigo by train. That way, you boys would be watching him instead of me. But you were too smart for him, Bat, old son. You figured it out that I was stringing along with Drummond."

"But he gave you the horse?"

"Shucks, no," Rowdy said. "Say, looking back on it now, I'm not so sure that Clee Drummond trusts me very far. He wouldn't tell me why that horse was so valuable, and he wouldn't give me the horse. Not right off. He put it in the mail to himself, care of general delivery, at Latigo. If you boys kept him from getting to Latigo pronto, I was to pick up the horse at the post office and keep it till Drummond could get in touch with me. The town marshal mailed it for him this morning. You boys should have watched that town marshal, too. The horse was in a mail sack on that train you boarded. Too bad. So near and yet so far."

The sudden silence that followed Rowdy's speech was so loud that it hurt his ears. Nearby, one of the ground-anchored horses pawed impatiently; a coal exploded in the fire, and the wind stirred music out of the pine tops. But no man spoke for a long minute, and no man moved. Then Bat Stull was quivering with anger.

"Twice now you've made a fool out of me, Dow," he said. "You did it in that Jubilee hotel, and you've did it again. I'm gonna ram this gun-barrel down your throat!"

"And fix it so I can't talk?" Rowdy observed. "Think twice! Bat, I did you a favour. If I'd told you on the train that the china horse was up in the next car in a mail pouch, you might have been excited enough to go after it. Fooling with the mail is a bad offence. Gets federal men riled up."

"Come on," Stull said hoarsely. "We're going on to Latigo. I'll get that stallion yet!"

"What's the all-fired rush?" Rowdy asked. "We've time for another cup of coffee."

Stull booted the coffee pot off the fire and sent it arcing through the air. Stumpy Grampis, a man thoroughly enjoying himself despite the tenseness of the moment, hee-hawed loudly. "Hospitality's gone from these hills," he decided. "Rowdy, we've done outworn our welcome."

"Nothing's changed for you two," Stull told them angrily. "You're coming along. The only reason I'm not taking your hides off is that you may be useful yet!"

Again they were up into saddles, but they were out of

them soon, for they'd found the trail that climbed to the top of Latigo Pass, and the Jubilee hostler had been on the conservative side when he'd stated that the horse that could make the hump had to be kin to a mountain goat. A little eagle blood in equine ancestry would have served better. The trail crawled up beyond the timber line, skirting a steep wall and narrowing down to next to nothing; and eternity was always at the left elbows of the toiling men. Sometimes they could glimpse the railroad tracks below them, two threads of steel twining in and out of a chaos of timber. The air grew colder and there were wisps of fog about the higher peaks.

"Brr-r-r!" Stumpy complained and made some reference to the ears of brass monkey.

The rest remained silent; they were saving their breath for the ascent, all except Stonehead Jackson, who began reeling off some aimless conversation that must have made very little sense, even on the occasion when he'd first heard it. They reached the crest and paused here, panting and heaving. The afternoon was far gone, and it was beginning to drizzle, a cold, relentless rain. Someone made talk of a fire, but a driving impatience was upon Bat Stull. He cursed them into motion again, and they began the descent.

It was the trail they'd followed, only in reverse. Again they had the cliff above them and a thousand feet of emptiness below, but the going was a little easier. In an hour they'd dropped down to a broader ledge where they could mount, and in another hour they were on a gentler slope, and here they found a wagon road. On a clear day, Latigo Basin would have been spreading beneath them at this point, but the rain made a sullen curtain, and the night was closing in fast.

"Look yonder," someone called and pointed through the trees to where a huge, shadowy house hid deep in the screening timber. "Now who in thunder would build away up here on the side of a hill?"

"That," Rowdy said solemnly, "is the home of the galoot who made a better mousetrap. He figured that folks would beat a path to his door, and, sure enough, we did."

But he was glad when the house had fallen from view. There was something very uninviting about that house, something that hinted of creaking doors and banging shutters and stairs that echoed when no one walked upon them. It was a house in keeping with the day—dark and gloomy and forbidding. Rowdy decided that a ghost would likely die of sheer loneliness in a place like that.

This far side of the mountain had been terraced by nature into a series of shelves with gentle slopes between them, and the wagon road wound ever downward. In the last daylight they came almost to the basin's floor, and here the timber thinned to intermittent clumps. And here, a few miles below the only other habitation they'd seen, they found a second building, or rather three, for the bigger one had two small structures behind it. A bell surmounted the largest building, and someone said, "A schoolhouse!"

"Kids have gone home for the night," another observed.

"Let's light and stretch the stiffness out of ourselves," the man nearest Stull suggested. "There's a stove inside, likely. And I could eat."

"So could I," Rowdy said.

Bat Stull frowned. His eyes were sweeping what could be seen of the basin, and, far to the south and below them, a few lights twinkled. That would be Latigo town, Rowdy judged. Stull said, "O.K., boys. We'll need a roof over our heads to-night. This is it."

Rowdy and Stumpy alighted with the rest and put their horses at the school-yard hitchrail. Across the towering miles, Rowdy had acted as though he were having the time of his life, yet he'd maintained a perpetual vigilance that had been hidden behind his flippant attitude. His gun and Stumpy's had been collected on the train, and those guns were now in the belt of the man who'd taken them. And there were suspicious eyes upon the captive pair at all times. Little chance of making a play for freedom under such circumstances, but Rowdy was still waiting. Maybe his moment was coming.

And he'd have to get a tail-hold on opportunity when it reared itself. He'd bluffed Bat Stull to a fare-you-well; he'd pretended a light-hearted indifference to the seriousness of his situation, but Bat Stull, growing increasingly desperate, was likewise growing increasingly dangerous. When Stull took to boarding trains, masked and armed, then Stull was gambling high. The man who'd always played safe was no longer playing safe. Therein lay Rowdy's peril, and Stumpy's too.

The outfit dismounted, they came trooping to the school-house door. It was locked, but at a word from Stull, Stone-head Jackson threw his massive shoulder against it, and the door capitulated, revealing a wide room with precise rows of desks and a larger desk at the far end. There was a pot-bellied stove, and it was still warm, and a fire was quickly stirred to life. Somebody got the bacon to sizzling, and the coffee pot, its shape forever ruined by Stull's angry kick, began bubbling.

"I like travelling with you boys," Rowdy said when the food was passed around. "You eat well—and often."

But his good humour wrung no like response from Bat Stull, for Stull was munching his food in the preoccupied manner of a man with a great deal on his mind. Putting down his coffee cup, Stull said, "You've been laughing ever since we took you off that train, Dow. You won't for long. I'm riding into Latigo to-night, and I'm getting the mail, even if the postmaster has to be hauled out of bed. And it had better be the right kind of mail!"

"Stonehead," Rowdy said. "You've been in the pen. Tell the big boss what it's like. He'll want to know, once he goes tampering with somebody else's mail."

But Stull grinned triumphantly. "I thought the whole deal out while we was coming over the hump," he said. "It won't be *me* that collects the mail. It will be Stumpy Grampis. Fact is, I won't be near him at the time. I'll just ride as far as the edge of Latigo with him."

Rowdy winked at his partner. "Stumpy," he said, "doesn't it make you feel proud the way Bat trusts you?"

"I ain't trustin' him," Stull said. "He wouldn't give me the sweat offen his nose. But *you're* staying here, Dow, and all my boys will stick around to watch you. Either Stumpy and me come ridin' back stirrup to stirrup, or Stumpy hits the grit. If I come back alone, you'll be a gone gosling after I show back. I reckon Stumpy will keep that in mind when I let him loose on his own at the edge of town."

Stull glared at Stumpy. "Git that coffee down you," he ordered. "We're riding."

Stumpy cast an eloquent, questioning look at Rowdy, but Rowdy could only grin, even though his heart wasn't in it. Stull went clumping down an aisle towards the ravaged door, Stumpy trailing behind him, and at the threshold Stull paused. "You boys keep Dow entertained," he said. "I don't want him to get tired of your company. He's got to be here when I get back."

Then he was gone, and Stumpy was gone with him, and Rowdy was alone with a circle of hostile faces—and with the reflection that this was a fine how-do-you-do. For there certainly was no china stallion reposing in the Latigo post office, as Bat Stull was going to shortly discover.

5. Latigo

LATIGO TOWN IN DIVERS RESPECTS was a twin to Jubilee, across the hump, and, for that matter, it bore a family resemblance to a hundred other hamlets in the mountain country. There was the same single-mindedness in the structures, the same straggly row of false fronts, the same superfluous number of saloons per capita. But Latigo had certain claims to individuality as well, the chief of these being a three figure population, not counting dogs, and the fact that it was the administrative seat of Latigo County, an expanse of acreage which encompassed the basin. This gave the town the right to a courthouse, a two-storeyed brick structure sumptuous enough to bring a glow of civic pride to the lowliest saloon swamper. The courthouse squatted in an expanse of shaggy lawn, and smack in the centre of this oasis stood a brass cannon, variously reported as having seen service in the ruckus with Mexico and the war between the States.

Also, Latigo had a complete set of county officials, for obviously it made no sense to build a courthouse and leave it empty. These officials came in various sizes and shapes, and prominent among them, though not by virtue of obesity, was Sheriff Ethelbert Pickens. Since that worthy was afflicted with a given name that had sent him in frantic search of a soubriquet at an early age, and since he was so thin that rumour maintained he could wear a double-barrelled shotgun for a pair of drawers, it was inevitable that he should be known as "Slim" Pickens.

Two things were a ritual with Slim Pickens. He was always the first man on the depot platform when the train came chugging into Latigo from the east, fetching the mail, and he always burned the midnight kerosene in his little shack on the town's outskirts the evening after the mail's arrival. For Slim Pickens was a man of unquenchable ambition, a man determined to perfect himself at the art of law enforcement, and he had clipped a coupon. Thus, for the past six months, he had been enrolled at the Acme School of Detecting and Criminology which provided a correspondence course for such students as Ethelbert Pickens who were situated back of beyond.

This course, laboriously and conscientiously pursued by Pickens, had given him more knowledge of criminal psychology, the art of shadowing, and the merits of the Bertillon system of identification than was good for a man of his intellect to possess. Also, the Acme people had furnished him with a make-up kit, for the seventeenth lesson had laid great stress on the value of disguise in tracking desperate characters to their dark and musty lairs. Slim Pickens had himself a time with that make-up kit.

In the late afternoon, when Bat Stull and his men, with Rowdy Dow and Stumpy Grampis as captives, were wending their way down the slope into Latigo Basin, Slim Pickens was putting in an impatient appearance at the depot, and, since Pickens was no man to waste an opportunity, he was at the same time testing the efficiency of a disguise. The usual clothes, from boots to Stetson, clad his emaciated body, but he'd donned a full beard, a magnificent moustache, and a wig which made a flowing show of hair beneath his hat. Latigo, used to such spectacles, had watched his progress to the depot in stony silence, and that had put satisfaction in Slim Pickens. But the train was late, and he discovered that he wasn't first to the platform to-day.

John Crenshaw, Latigo's banker-rancher, was also waiting for the train. A big man, red of face and bushy of eyebrows, Crenshaw's garb was indicative of the two pursuits which occupied his time and his energy—the cattle ranch in the basin, and the bank he'd built here in town upon a foundation of faith, and very little else. He wore a black business suit, and a ponderous watch chain crossed his vest, but his trousers were tucked into worn boots, and his sombrero had withstood a good deal of weather. A self-contained man, he had a mouth that was made for laughing, and eyes that had looked into the hearts of men and seen there frailty and

greed, but also an essential goodness. He waited now with
patience; he had learned patience across the stony years.
When the sheriff appeared, Crenshaw smiled and said,
"Howdy, Slim."

"You know me?" Pickens queried in utter disappointment.

"Why not?" Crenshaw countered. "You're wearing your
sheriff's star on your vest."

Pickens looked down in astonishment and quickly transferred the betraying tin to the inside of his vest. Crenshaw
gazed toward the mountain tops and said, "Rain up there.
And it looks like it's moving this way. That will probably
make the train later than usual."

"Listen!" Pickens said. "She just blew her whistle at the
mile sign."

"And Thane Buckmaster's aboard," Crenshaw decided.
"Here comes Curly Bill Callaghan, his foreman, to pick him
up and haul him to the Eagle's Eyrie. Slim, will you tell me
why a man who runs no cattle and has no crew needs a
foreman?"

Toward the depot had come a handsome, black surrey,
drawn by a pair of matched blacks, blooded horses that
might have graced a king's stable. The man who alighted
was not so regal. A huge, solid-shouldered fellow with a
prominent jaw and a hard and petulant look to him, he wore
range garb, and his sombrero lay upon his back, held in
place by the throat latch, for Curly Bill Callaghan was
inordinately vain about the thatch that had given him his
soubriquet. Slim Pickens frowned as he watched Callaghan
carefully tie the team to a gnawed hitchrail.

"Buckmaster's cowless ranch isn't the only queer thing
about the jigger," Pickens observed. "Why should a man
want to perch halfway up a mountain when there's plenty of
bottom land he could buy? Blazes, he's got three-quarters of
the basin under his thumb now. All he's got to do is wait
until option time is up and he'll be picking up ranches left
and right."

Crenshaw shrugged. "If that's what he intends to do. One
of these days he'll be showing his cards. And I'm not sure
it will be a happy day for Latigo Basin."

The train emerged out of the lowering mist and came
chuffing triumphantly toward the depot. The horses that had

hauled Thane Buckmaster's fancy rig down from his mountain home began rearing frantically, and Curly Bill Callaghan fought at them with a cruel and masterful hand. Then the train was grinding to a stop, and the single coach began disgorging its passengers. The tobacco drummer was the first to alight, and he quickly hurried away. Logan MacLean stepped down next and paused to lend a hand to a very pretty girl and her veiled companion. These three were strangers to Latigo and strangers to John Crenshaw, and the banker's eyes were without interest until the tall, bare-headed man with the cape came down to the platform. Slim Pickens had headed toward the baggage car to personally oversee the delivery of the mail sack, and Crenshaw crossed quickly to the man in the cape, reaching him a step behind Curly Bill Callaghan.

"Howdy, boss," Callaghan said. "Have a good trip?"

Crenshaw brushed past Callaghan and extended his hand. "Glad to see you back, Buckmaster. But if I'd known you were gone, I'd have saved myself a jaunt up to the Eagle's Eyrie the other day. Your foreman, here, was mighty myste- rious about your whereabouts, but he finally admitted that you'd likely be on this train."

"The mystery was uncalled for," Buckmaster said in a clipped, precise voice. "As you know, I was appointed chairman of the Latigo County Fair this year. I went east on business for the fair. We'll have an exceptional show this fall. I've provided for a carnival and a balloon ascension act that will bring folks here from half of Montana. The show equipment should be in on to-morrow's freight."

Crenshaw's smile was grim. "Considering the off-season we've had, the Latigo ranchers may not be in a mood for anything so extravagant. But I haven't been waiting for you on that account. I want to know if you've reconsidered. You've got a blanket option on a string of ranches. I'd like to take it off your hands."

"This is hardly the place to talk business," Buckmaster said.

"I'm getting too old to climb mountains every day," Crenshaw countered pointedly. "Will you sell, or won't you?"

"You have the cash?"

Crenshaw frowned. "I can give you paper for paper and a fair margin of profit will be in the deal."

Buckmaster's graven face darkened. "Look, Crenshaw," he said. "I'm a business man, the same as yourself. Ten years ago I came here from the East with enough money to indulge a few whims of my own—the Eagle's Eyrie being one of them. I was taken for considerable of a fool by most of the citizenry. Yet I've prospered. I went into the business of loaning money, and I offered it at less interest than your bank demands, and with less insistence on collateral. Very well, I've gotten a blanket option on a group of ranches. Now you want to buy it. All I ask is cash on the barrelhead before I consider selling it—which I'm not likely to do. But when you have the cash, come and talk to me."

Temper tugged hard at Crenshaw and glinted in his eyes. "You've told it straight, Buckmaster, but you've left out one thing," he said. "The human element. I know these people; I saw this basin grow. I built a bank here with no more capital than a pair of hands and a big idea. I've had setbacks. When my bank was really beginning to grow, I lost one hundred thousand dollars in a stage robbery. I mortgaged my ranch to keep my bank from going under, because a lot of people were depending upon that bank. It's taken me ten years to recuperate, and I'm still running on the ragged edge of nothing. No wonder people found it easier to borrow from you! But, frankly, I'm suspicious of what you intend doing with that option. What happens to the ranchers who were foolish enough to give you an option on their ranches and their futures when the day comes that they can't pay back and have to sell out to you?"

Buckmaster said, "What do you do when paper falls due?"

"I size up the man, not the potentialities of high profit. If he's worth backing, I string along with him, even though it pinches."

Buckmaster said, "And the very men you back have gotten suspicious of you. Don't you know that they're whispering that your bank isn't sound? Crenshaw, you're a fool!"

Crenshaw's fist doubled, and about him now was the look of a man who had been pressed too far. "If there's a whispering campaign, you started it, Buckmaster!" he snapped. Curly Bill Callaghan's hand fell to the forty-five at his hip, and Buckmaster's foreman said, "Better forget it, Crenshaw. The boss is tired. And he's told you how he stands. Come up and see him when you've got the hard, jingling stuff that makes good talking."

Crenshaw turned away; it was that or plant his fist in Buckmaster's face and risk whatever retaliation Callaghan would make. And turning aside, he saw the girl and her companion standing amidst their luggage. The girl's blue eyes were upon him, and there was an appeal in them, and Crenshaw crossed over to her and doffed his sombrero.

"You're strangers here, I'd judge," he said. "Can I be of service?"

"If there's a good hotel here," the girl said, "I'd appreciate being directed to it."

Crenshaw led her to the end of the platform and pointed along Latigo's erratic street. "The Empire is the only one we've got. You'll find it satisfactory."

Logan MacLean had been holding some sort of consultation with the conductor, and he appeared now, hat in hand. "If I can help," he said, "I'll be glad to. How about my taking your luggage?"

John Crenshaw looked at this pair and remembered his own youth, and he said, "Go ahead, young man. These ladies wish to put up at the Empire." And then, because he was a considerate man, he withdrew and went about his business. Curly Bill Callaghan was helping Thane Buckmaster into the surrey, and Crenshaw frowned in their direction and then turned into the street. Meanwhile Logan MacLean still stood with his hat bunched in his hands, mesmerised by a pair of blue eyes.

"You going to be here long?" he blurted.

The girl said, "Perhaps. My mother is trying to locate an old friend who used to ranch in this basin. Sam Usher, by name."

"I'm a stranger myself," MacLean said. "But I'd sure like to help you look for this Usher fellow."

The girl said, "You're very kind. I saw you watching me on the train. Please don't think me rude because I haven't been as responsive as I might have. Mother and I have only recently suffered a loss. I'm sure you understand."

He said, "Why that's all right, Miss——"

"Jones," she said. "It's unbelievable, isn't it? But then there are really a lot of people named Jones."

"Sure," he said. "That's right. There are. Now if you'll let me take that luggage."

"There isn't much, and I can manage," said Miss Jones. "But if you'd really like to do me a favour, you may. I heard what you said aboard the train about being a railroad man when those awful fellows appeared at that water tank and took those two men away with them. Frankly, I'm worried about that. Couldn't you report the matter to the authorities here and see that something is done? Perhaps a posse could be sent out."

Logan MacLean had been discussing that very subject with the conductor just a few minutes before, and it had been MacLean's intention to contact Latigo's law just as quickly as he took care of the more pressing matter of attending to the comfort of this girl. Now he frowned, and then he had to grin at his own thought. Why in blazes hadn't he kicked up more of a rumpus when those masked men had boarded the train? Maybe he might have goaded one of them into slamming a fist into his face. Now that would have been something! For young Logan MacLean could think of nothing nicer at the moment than having Miss Jones as concerned over his welfare as she apparently was over the fate of the two men who'd been taken from the train.

6. Stumpy Stumped

STUMPY GRAMPIS, RIDING AWAY from the Latigo school-house with Bat Stull at his side, was not the happiest man in the world. The miles that stretched to Latigo town proved to be long and muddy and of unsound footing, Stull was an untalkative companion, and the rain drizzled monotonously, seeping through Stumpy's clothes and finding holes in his ancient hat and running down his back. This condition made him exceedingly uncomfortable, and his irritation turned him morose and savage. Stumpy was no duck.

The lights of Latigo played a perverse game of continually eluding them, and it seemed that they were on the trail forever. After the first hour, the rain dwindled to nothing, and a sickly moon showed itself to risk a look at the soggy earth. But Stumpy's saddle was still wet, and his spirits were in no way brightened. For Stumpy was a man possessed of both a damp posterior and a worried mind.

Actually, his situation seemed simple enough. He was to go into Latigo and arouse the postmaster and demand mail designated for Clee Drummond. With a glib enough story, he'd doubtless be given the mail, and Stumpy had a persuasive tongue. Meanwhile, Rowdy Dow was being held as hostage by Bat Stull's men. If the mail proved to be satisfactory to the extent that it included a china stallion worth one hundred thousand round iron men, Bat Stull would return to the schoolhouse in high good humour and might even be content to release both Stumpy and Rowdy. But if the proper mail wasn't forthcoming, Bat Stull was going to be mighty angry. In which case somebody would likely get hurt. And the fly in the soup was that the china stallion certainly wasn't reposing in Latigo's post office.

No, sir. That little old horse was elsewhere—and elsewhere might be a danged hard spot to locate this moist evening. Rowdy Dow had made a fool out of Bat Stull twice lately, but Rowdy, in the long run, had merely talked himself out of the frying pan and smack into the fire. Therefore it behooved Stumpy Grampis to get his horny old hands on that toy horse, or Rowdy Dow was going to be feeling the blaze before very long.

But there was hope. A man had a lot of time for thinking on a trail like this one, and, by grab, Stumpy Grampis wasn't letting any moss gather on his grey matter. Maybe, if he was reasoning right and if he was lucky, he'd ride back with Bat Stull to-night after all. And with that china stallion delivered into Stull's eager hands. Turning the stallion over to Stull would be as bitter a chore as drinking alkali water out of a stale hoofprint, but there wasn't much choice. Not with Rowdy's life, and perhaps his own, hanging in the balance. One hundred thousand bucks was a heap of money to fling away in one evening, but it certainly wouldn't buy a feller a new suit of skin.

But first Stumpy had to get his hands on the missing china stallion. . . .

More miles unreeled, and they cornered the will o' the wisp at last; they had lost the lights of Latigo many times, but they rounded a bluff to find the town before them. It was nearly midnight, Latigo's gayest hour, and even on the outskirts they could hear the roar of the saloons. Riders from basin ranches, mindful that sun-up meant rolling out of the soogans, were making their departures in twos and threes. Bat Stull reined short in the shadow of a giant cottonwood and indicated that Stumpy was to do likewise. And here Stull broke his long silence.

"You're on your own now, Grampis," Stull said. "You can ride on into town—and you can ride through it, if you've a mind to, and maybe I'll never see your homely old face again. But just keep remembering Rowdy Dow, meanwhile. Or maybe you're thinking of picking up a gun somewhere and giving me the slip and heading back to the schoolhouse to pull a rescue. My boys will be expecting some such damn' fool play as that. Or you can take your tale to the law and maybe get a posse to follow you to the schoolhouse. Any way you work it, the first cap that's cracked will be aimed at Rowdy Dow.''

Stumpy sullenly said, "Save yore wind, mister. I know when I'm grabbed where the hair's short.''

"I'll wait here an hour," Stull continued. "You'll likely need that much time to find where the postmaster lives and get him out of bed and persuade him to open the post office. I don't care how you work that trick; it's up to you. But if you don't show back at the end of an hour, I'll figger you're trying to run some kind of sandy. I'll be heading for the schoolhouse then.''

"I hope tuh hell," said Stumpy, "that it starts raining again and the water comes up to your ears!''

"One hour," Stull said emphatically.

Whereupon Stumpy jogged the horse that Stull had loaned him and went riding into Latigo. He came along the main street with his eyes alert for a certain establishment, but he passed the post office without a sideward glance and alighted before the depot. Here a youngish man, his face turned sickly green by the eyeshade he wore, hunched over a telegraph key. The fellow started nervously when Stumpy appeared in the doorway, but Stumpy smiled a snaggle-toothed smile and said, "Howdy, bub. Train come in this afternoon?''

"It did," said the telegrapher, turning away from his instrument.

"You see the passengers light down from it?''

"I'd just come on duty then.''

"I was lookin' for a mighty pretty gal and her mother. The old one was wearin' a black dress and veil.''

"Those ladies got off here," the telegrapher assured him and eyed Stumpy quizzically. "Say, you're not related to them, are you?''

"The mother," Stumpy lied glibly, "is an old sweetheart o' mine. Now that she's shovelled her husband under, I reckoned I might come callin' again. Where'll I find 'em, bub?''

"If they stayed in town, they likely put up at the hotel. We've only got one. The Empire. You'll find it up the street.''

"Thanks," said Stumpy. "So long, now. Gotta hurry. Ain't got many more years to waste.''

Mounted again, he rode back up the street, this time looking for the hotel, and he found it without trouble. In a lobby that was much like the one in the Mountain View in Jubilee, he approached the desk clerk.

"You got a mother and daughter registered here?" he demanded. "Come in on to-day's train."

The clerk spun the register around. "Here they are," he said. "Number four. Upstairs." Stumpy, peering hard, saw the scrawled names; they looked like so many hen-tracks, but a man could decipher them if he worked hard at it. They read: "Mrs. B. R. Jones and daughter," but the address which followed was a blot.

"That's them," he decided. "They up in their room?"

"They haven't left it," the clerk said. "Had their supper sent up to them just about dark." He gave Stumpy a longer look, and Stumpy was quite an eyeful. The rain had made a soggy ruin of his sombrero, his boots were scuffed and muddy, and he'd forgotten the last time he'd shaved, it had been so long ago. "You sure they want to see *you?*" the clerk asked suspiciously.

"I," Stumpy Grampis said stiffly, "am the family lawyer. They're expecting me."

Whereupon he went climbing up the stairs to march along an upper hallway in search of number four. And a high elation was in him, for Lady Luck had been at his elbow, and things were breaking better than he'd hoped. But when he found the room he sought and had a look through the open doorway, the spirits went out of him. Mrs. Jones and her daughter had had visitors. Rude visitors. For the room was completely topsy-turvy, the scanty furniture disarranged, and all the signs said that somebody had staged a free-for-all with no holds barred. And the room was empty of people.

For a moment Stumpy stood staring. He had followed a trail, and this was the end of it. He had based a hope and a scheme on a series of remembrances, and the first had been of Rowdy Dow receiving that confounded china stallion from Clee Drummond in the Jubilee jailhouse. Rowdy had taken the tiny figurine in his hand, contemplated its size and fragility, and placed it in the crown of his sombrero. It had been inside that same sombrero when Rowdy and Stumpy had walked into their hotel room in Jubilee to find Bat Stull and Stonehead Jackson waiting for them. That was why Rowdy had been careful to keep his sombrero on when he'd shaved, a procedure which had aroused Stull's curiosity at the time. By grab, that had been a bad moment when Stull had noticed the sombrero!

All this Stumpy had remembered and had turned over in his mind on the long trail from the schoolhouse into Latigo to-night. Rowdy Dow had been searched by Stull and his men after the pair of them had been removed from the train on the other side of Latigo Pass. No china stallion had been found, and that had puzzled Stumpy as much as it had disappointed Stull's crew, though Stumpy had realised that it was neither the time nor the place to plague Rowdy with questions. But since then Stumpy had figured out the answers for himself.

Rowdy had removed his sombrero only once since he'd placed that china stallion within it. That had been aboard the train, when he'd doffed it and made a sweeping bow to Miss Jones and apologised for the presence of Stull and his men. Which meant that Rowdy had at the same time dumped the china stallion into the lap of Miss Jones, doing so with his back to Bat Stull, who hadn't seen that little play. And Miss Jones had been discreet enough to make no sign that anything significant had happened. Doubtless Miss Jones had not been deaf to the loud demands Bat Stull had made for that same china stallion just a few minutes before Rowdy had turned the tiny horse over to her. Miss Jones had understood Rowdy's intent and co-operated. A smart girl, that Miss Jones. And pretty, too.

That was why Stumpy, upon leaving Bat Stull on Latigo's outskirts, not so very long ago, had gone directly in search of Miss Jones, though he hadn't known her name then. Miss Jones would doubtless remember him as Rowdy's companion aboard the train, and Miss Jones, he'd hoped, would surrender the china stallion. All that would remain to be done then would be to turn it over to Stull. But Miss Jones, meanwhile, had obviously been persuaded to leave the hotel, and the persuasion had been violent. Thus had the trail petered out, and thus were Stumpy's hopes blasted.

Then he became conscious that someone had climbed the stairs and was hurrying down the hall. Stumpy spun around to find himself confronted by the young man who'd sat across the aisle from Miss Jones and her mother aboard the train, and with this young man, Logan MacLean, was a tall, cadaverous person with a sheriff's star upon his vest. Also the lawman had a gun. It was in his hand.

The sheriff said, "Here's one of 'em now, I reckon! Come back to the scene of the crime. They always do."

"Wait!" MacLean ejaculated. "I know this fellow! He's one of the two that was taken off the train. Remember, I told you about them this afternoon?"

Stumpy said, "Will somebody tell me what brought you two hot-footin' it up here?"

MacLean said, "My name's Logan MacLean. I'm with the railroad. I called on Miss Jones and her mother about fifteen minutes ago and found them gone and saw the signs of a struggle in the room. I dashed out at once and fetched Sheriff Pickens. Who are you, mister?"

"Grampis is the name," Stumpy said. "Tell this here lawdog to put that cannon away before it goes off and scares hell outa somebody. You heard what was said on the train about a china stallion. My pard managed to give it to Miss Jones afore we was hauled off that train. Me, I come to git it."

"So far as I know, he's talking straight, Sheriff," MacLean said.

Slim Pickens reluctantly pouched his gun. "I take it you didn't stop at the desk after you found the ladies missing," he said to MacLean. "Maybe the clerk saw them leave."

"I asked at the desk," Stumpy volunteered. "The clerk claimed they were still in the room."

"Then they were taken down the rear stairway," Slim Pickens announced triumphantly. "That's what we call the process of elimination. Come on, we'll look for clues."

Stumpy cast a last glance into the disordered room. No sense in searching it for the china stallion; he was beginning to suspect that there might be a strong connection between Miss Jones's possession of the little horse and her subsequent disappearance. That meant that whoever had spirited off Miss Jones and her mother had likely taken the figurine as well.

Slim Pickens was proceeding down the hall with his nose as close to the carpet as he could get it, and Stumpy and Logan MacLean trailed unenthusiastically behind. Pickens suddenly seized upon some object and cried, "Mud! That means that someone came up the back stairs from the alley. Fellers, we're making progress!"

A door gave into a covered stairway that clung to the rear of the building, a narrow flight of steps as dark as a sheepherder's hopes of winning a cowtown election. They went down these stairs in single file and came to an abrupt stop in an alleyway where Pickens got a match aglow and had a look around. Disappointment turned his thin face bleak before the match burned out.

"Tracks a-plenty," he said. "Too many. A dozen riders have probably gone up and down this alley since nightfall."

"You mean you can't trail the kidnappers?" MacLean asked with considerable concern.

"We could get horses and cut for sign," Pickens said mournfully. "But likely the rain's washed out anything that might help us. Gents, we're up against a blank wall."

It was obvious that so far there'd been nothing in the correspondence course of the Acme School of Detecting and Criminology to cover a situation like this. But Stumpy Grampis had a right to be the most disappointed of the three. Slim Pickens was concerned with a crime that had been perpetrated practically under his nose. Logan MacLean was worried about the whereabouts of Miss Jones. But Stumpy Grampis had Rowdy Dow to think about, for there'd be no turning a china stallion over to Bat Stull this night.

7. Meeting at Midnight

ROWDY DOW, LEFT at the Latigo schoolhouse with Bat Stull's men while that worthy went riding to town with Stumpy Grampis, faced a long and unentertaining evening. Under other circumstances, he might have felt flattered that Stull had elected to go alone with Stumpy, leaving the full force of his crew to keep alert eyes upon Rowdy, but there was little satisfaction in that reflection. His chances at escape were slimmer than the shadow of a lodgepole pine, and he needed desperately to escape. For there was going to be the merry blue blazes to pay when Bat Stull came riding back.

Yes, it was a situation to bring the sweat out on a man, but Rowdy kept his concern from showing. He'd bluffed Stull and his men this far by a display of gaiety that made him seem the most carefree man in the world, and bluff was the only weapon left in his armament. That, and an agile brain. Seating himself behind the teacher's desk, he hoisted his legs to its littered top and crossed them comfortably. Stull's men had scattered themselves about the room in a thin semi-circle, hemming him in, and Stonehead Jackson, surprise of surprises, had dug a book out of a desk and was laboriously reading. From the scowl of concentration on Jackson's vacuous face, Rowdy judged the tome to be mighty heavy literature. But it proved to be a copy of the *Arabian Nights*.

After a half-hour, Jackson raised his furrowed brow. "Is this here stuff true?" he demanded of no one in particular.

"True as gospel," Rowdy assured him. "Took a trip to the coast once, and the first gent I saw on the streets of Seattle was Sinbad the Sailor."

Jackson closed the book on one huge index finger, and,

reaching out with his free hand, gingerly rubbed the lamp which had been placed on one of the children's desks. Nothing happened. "Aw, shucks!" Jackson said.

"Can't expect a genie to show up just any old time," Rowdy said consolingly. "Those big fellows get mighty independent when they're in a mood to be ornery."

Jackson went back to the book, and the silence descended again, broken only by the fidgeting of the men and certain low-voiced and desultory conversations, and the thin drumming of rain on the roof. Rowdy, lost in thought, was beginning to see the shape of an inspiration. He looked at these men and wondered if his idea would work, and he saw them as of a pattern, lesser satellites of Bat Stull, men who were greedy and suspicious and short of the courage it took to be the sort of outlaw Rowdy Dow had been.

Rowdy began laughing then, softly at first, as a man will who is enjoying a joke he doesn't intend sharing with others. Someone looked up irritably and said, "If there's anything funny around here, it must be on my blind side."

Rowdy said, "I've just been thinking how easy Bat is getting away with this. You know, I had the notion that Bat was a little on the stupid side. Until to-night."

"Getting away with what?" Two men asked it at once.

"Look," said Rowdy, "has he told any of you the name of the man Butch Rafferty turned a hundred thousand dollars over to years ago—the gent who's going to hand that money back when he sees the china stallion?"

Stull's men looked at each other blankly, and then one said, "Supposing he hasn't? Bat got the yarn from Stonehead, here, who heard everything that was said between Butch Rafferty and Clee Drummond in the prison hospital. Bat knows that Stonehead could tell us the same story. How about it, Jackson? Who *was* the rancher who kept Rafferty's loot for him?"

Jackson, deeply absorbed in the *Thousand and One Nights,* waved a gigantic hand. "Go away," he said absently.

Rowdy began laughing again. "What's the difference if you do find out? You still have to have the stallion to collect the dinero. And you haven't got it. No, sir. Bat Stull's the boy who's gone to lay his hands on that little horse."

"Meaning what?" one demanded belligerently.

"Meaning that Stull outsmarted the bunch of did he leave *all* of you here to watch me when any have done the job?"

Thus did Rowdy plant the seed, and in this fert... basin anything grew. For a long moment the six sat with pleated foreheads, looking, in such a setting, like so many school-boys caught with their lessons unprepared. And of the six, Stonehead Jackson, avidly following the fortunes of Aladdin, was the only one who was obviously not thinking of Bat Stull. One, a squat individual whose hairline almost met his eyebrows, came suddenly out of his seat and started toward the door.

"Me, I'm ridin' after Bat," he said emphatically.

But the scrawny man whom Stumpy Grampis had met so violently behind the Mountain View Hotel in Jubilee was as quick to come to a stand. "Get back here, Luke!" he ordered. "Can't you see what this slick-tongued jigger is trying to do? He aims to stampede us into lighting out after Bat and forgetting all about *him!* Don't fall for his fool talk."

"Sure, sit down, Luke," Rowdy urged. "In a little while Bat will have the china stallion. Then he'll head to a certain basin ranch pronto and pick up the money. He's an impatient cuss, Bat is. But don't you worry. As soon as Bat has those hundred thousand dollars, he'll tote 'em back and split 'em up seven ways." Rowdy paused and winked solemnly. "You'd do the same for Bat, now wouldn't you?"

Again they were silent, Luke standing hesitantly in the aisle, the others hunkered into seats that were too small for them. And Rowdy, sensing the workings of their minds, saw triumph almost within his grasp. Each was measuring Bat Stull with the yardstick of his own individuality, each was thinking what he, himself, would do if he came upon that hundred thousand dollars alone, and even the scrawny man who had sensed Rowdy's intent was doing some deep thinking. Only Stonehead Jackson remained unperturbed. Running out his tongue, which looked for all the world like a razor strop, the giant wet a finger and carefully turned a page.

Luke broke the silence with a curse. His little eyes roved to the four corners of the room, and then he advanced toward Rowdy, but he skirted the teacher's desk and tested a door that was placed between the blackboards and behind Rowdy. The door gave to Luke's touch, and he vanished into darkness, but he reappeared again quickly.

"Place in here where the kids leave their coats and hats," he announced. "It only has this one door, and there's a key for it." He tested the lock quickly. "Let's shove Dow inside and lock him up and leave Jackson to keep an eye on him."

They were quick enough to get the idea. "Come to think of it," said the scrawny man, "Bat might run into trouble in Latigo. Chances are he'll be glad to have us show up."

Thus was the balance swung. Luke crossed to Stonehead Jackson and shook the giant's shoulder roughly. "We're leaving you here to take care of things," Luke roared in Jackson's ear. "Read that damn' book if you want to, but just make sure that Dow stays where we put him. Let him get away, and we'll take the hide right off you!"

Rowdy was thrust into the cloak room and the door was shut and locked. From the room beyond the sounds of much movement percolated to him; soon the schoolhouse door banged shut; there was the creaking of saddle gear, the plop of hooves in the mud of the yard, and then silence. It had been as simple as that to sell Stull's men a bill of goods and send them after Bat Stull, but their suspicion had been tinged with scepticism, and they had played it safe. Rowdy had succeeded in getting rid of them, but he'd helped himself not at all. For he was just as much a prisoner as before. A locked door and Stonehead Jackson's presence as before. A sufficient number of factors to keep him here.

In fact, contemplating his situation in the darkness of the cloak room, Rowdy found it worse. Stull's men would overtake their leader, and they would find Stull with no china stallion to show for much wet riding. Whereupon they would realise that they'd been twice duped, and they'd return with a mighty anger spurring them. Any way Rowdy looked at it, it behooved him more than ever to get out of here.

But how? Rowdy remembered the skeleton key he'd been carrying—the one he'd meant to mail to the governor as a sign of good faith—but the key was gone. He'd had it in Jubilee, but he'd lost it since, probably when he'd been searched so thoroughly by Stull. He fell to examining the cloak room, feeling his way gingerly around the walls. There was no other door; Luke had been right about that. The rain ceased drumming on the roof, and when the sickly moon showed itself, Rowdy discovered a window. But it was set high in the wall and was entirely too small to accommodate his broad shoulders. He stood silent for a while, listening intently, but the only sound from the room beyond was the intermittent turning of pages as Stonehead Jackson delved deeper into Oriental fantasy.

Fishing out the makings, Rowdy built himself a cigarette, and, touching a match to it, contemplated whether it might be a good idea to set the building on fire. That would perhaps stir Jackson into unlocking the cloak room door, and then again, it might not. Rowdy decided against such a move.

He seated himself on the floor to think things out, and, in doing so, he found a hard object beneath him. It proved to be a corked beer bottle, and Rowdy recognised it with surprise. Either the pupils of this Latigo schoolhouse were a mature and debauched lot, or school teachers had acquired different tastes than when Rowdy had been a boy. Pulling the cork, he tilted the bottle, but there wasn't a drop left. Not one. He was about to fling the bottle away, figuring that all his luck had clabbered to-night, and then a new inspiration came to him.

Drawing hard on the cigarette, he expelled a mouthful of smoke into the bottle. Holding his thumb over the opening, he pulled at the cigarette again, and repeated the process of blowing the smoke into the bottle. From time to time he held the bottle up to the moonlight now trickling through the window. He built a number of cigarettes before he had enough smoke in the bottle to satisfy himself, and then he pushed the cork in hard. He was ready to flirt with Lady Luck again.

"Jackson!" he cried, coming to a stand and rattling the doorknob violently. "Let me out!"

"Go away," the giant mumbled. "Can't you see I'm busy reading?"

"*Jackson!*" Rowdy put panic into it. "I've got a genie in here. In a bottle!"

Silence. Dead silence. Then there came a slight movement which might have been Jackson hauling himself out of the cramped confines of the seat.

"Hurry!" Rowdy shouted. "He's a mean one. He might push the cork out any minute now!"

Footsteps. A big man lumbering across the floor. Rowdy held his breath, and then the key turned. Stumbling from the cloak room, the beer bottle in his hand, Rowdy held it up to the horrified eyes of Stonehead Jackson. Most of the smoke had settled in thick layers on the bottom of the bottle, but, up toward the neck, wisps swirled as Rowdy shook the bottle.

"A genie!" Jackson breathed. "You sure he's a mean one?"

"The ones in the brown bottles always are," Rowdy insisted. "Quick! Hand me your gun and I'll shoot him as he comes out! Before he gets too big to be bothered by a bullet!"

This was the moment when time treadmilled for Rowdy. If Jackson acted instinctively and obeyed, as he'd done when Rowdy had sent him down to the Mountain View lobby while Bat Stull lay unconscious in the Jubilee hotel, then the game was won. The giant's eyes were wide with horror; he had worked his way through a few books in his day, had Stonehead Jackson, but this was the first time one had ever come to life before his eyes. Like a man mesmerised, Jackson extended his gun to Rowdy, and Rowdy took the weapon with his free hand.

"Step back, Jackson!" he ordered. "The jigger may come out a-snorting and a-pawing!"

But there was a brain inside that thick skull of Jackson's. True, it wasn't much of a brain, and it was as sluggish as a bogged heifer, but it worked in its own fashion. For suddenly suspicion had replaced horror in Jackson's eyes, and the giant said, "Say, I'll betcha that's smoke in there. You're trying to fool me, that's what you're doing!"

He came at Rowdy then with his arms outstretched, and there was only one thing for Rowdy to do, and he did it. Hoisting the gun, he brought the barrel down so hard against Jackson's skull that Rowdy was sure he'd bent the shape out of the six-shooter. Jackson's eyes rolled upward until the whites showed, the giant's knees came unhinged, and he slumped to the floor.

Kneeling, Rowdy put his hand to the man's heart and was glad to find it still beating. Then, because the impulse was too great to be conquered, Rowdy dragged the unconscious giant to a sitting position against the wall, carefully folded Jackson's hands in the man's lap, and, picking up a dunce cap from a stool near the teacher's desk, Rowdy placed the cap on Jackson's head.

After which Rowdy went hurrying down the aisle and out of the building. There were only two horses left at the hitch-rack, and Rowdy picked the speedier looking. Swinging into the saddle, he thrust Jackson's gun into his belt, and, pointing the mount toward Latigo, Rowdy took the wagon road to town.

It was nearly midnight, he guessed, and if he was any good at reckoning time and distance, Bat Stull and Stumpy Grampis would likely be reaching town just about now. Stull's men, gone in search of their leader, had probably covered half the distance. Rowdy's immediate concern was for his old partner's safety, and he wanted to keep the horse at a high gallop, but he didn't dare. This road was full of holes, and the holes were full of rain water, and there were all the makings of a mean accident if a fellow wasn't careful.

He wished for more moonlight, but it was futile wishing. The road coiled down to the flat floor of the basin and then writhed toward Latigo, sometimes stretching like a silvery ribbon across the open land, and sometimes losing itself in those intermittent tree clumps which dotted the basin's floor.

Yet as arduous as this trail proved to be, Rowdy rode with elation, for he had a good horse beneath him and a gun close at hand, and Lady Luck had smiled after all. There was one chore yet to be done to round out the night, and that was to get Stumpy away from Stull's crowd. But Rowdy had formulated no plans. First he must get to Latigo, and then he'd see how the sign read.

A clump of trees swallowed him. Here only a little moonlight managed to filter down through the canopy of leaves, and Rowdy almost sent the horse smashing into an obstruction in the road before he became aware of it. A handsome surrey, drawn by a pair of matched blacks, had bogged down in a sea of mud, and there was moonlight enough to show Rowdy one man who stood by the roadside doing nothing, and another who toiled at freeing the rig. The one who worked was solid-shouldered and bare-headed, his sombrero hanging by its throat latch. He must have had a hatchet handy, for he'd stripped down a small tree, rolled a rock into place, and was using the tree as a lever to lift a rear wheel from the bog. The second man, shapeless beneath a cape and also bare-headed, merely watched.

All this Rowdy saw at a single glance, and he instantly recognised the watching man as the still-faced one who'd been aboard the train out of Jubilee. But there was something else that caught Rowdy's eye as he hauled to a stop. Two passengers sat in the back seat of the rig, and they aroused Rowdy's instant curiosity, for they were keeping their seats at a time when it was expedient to lighten the load. Then he realised that they were bound and gagged, and he also realised that he'd seen them both before.

One was the girl who'd sat ahead of him on the train; the other was the person he'd presumed was her mother. But the broad-brimmed hat and veil were gone now, and Rowdy's eyes widened. For the person in the black dress of a widow was obviously a man, a grey-faced man with a heavy moustache.

Even in this dim light, Rowdy thought he saw mute appeal in the girl's eyes, and that brought him out of the saddle, Stonehead Jackson's gun in his hand. "What in blazes is going on here?" he demanded.

The man who was trying to lever the rig out of the mudhole abruptly ceased his efforts, his hand starting toward the gun at his hip, and Rowdy took a quick step forward, his own gun tilting to cover the fellow. That was where Rowdy made his mistake. His movement had brought him almost abreast of the man in the cape, Thane Buckmaster, and he should have kept his eye on Buckmaster. He didn't see Buckmaster's hand come from under the cape. Not in time. He caught the dull flash of moonlight upon a descending gun-barrel, and he swerved quickly then, trying to swing Jackson's gun into play at the same time. But he moved too late. Buckmaster's gun-barrel caught him along the side of the head, and the lights went out for Rowdy Dow.

8. The Eagle's Eyrie

COMING BACK TO CONSCIOUSNESS, Rowdy wondered if he were dead, and decided that various sky-pilots had been telling it wrong about the hereafter. A man was supposed to get his dues in a place of eternal fire and brimstone, whereas Rowdy was both cold and wet, a condition further aggravated by the fact that someone was diligently swabbing his forehead with a damp bandanna. He did a little speculating about that—as much as a man could whose head was thundering like a Sioux war-drum—and the obvious conclusion was that he hadn't gone where the sky-pilots had always intimated he would go. The governor's pardon! That was it! The pardon had influenced the old St. Pete and got Rowdy through those pearly gates. Opening his eyes, he found himself cradled in a man's arms, and thus he learned that he was still alive. Rowdy had seen pictures of angels, and they didn't look like Stumpy Grampis.

It was Stumpy who'd soaked a bandanna in a puddle of rain water and was using it to restore Rowdy to mobility. Two other individuals hovered near Stumpy, and one, Logan MacLean, Rowdy recognised from the train. The other, a gent so thin that he could have climbed through a keyhole without scraping his elbows, wore a sheriff's star. Rowdy instantly felt for his gun. Such was the hold that habit made on a man. Then he remembered the pardon again. Potshooting at sheriffs was a thing of the past.

Stumpy said gleefully, "He's come awake. How you feeling, Rowdy, old hoss?"

Rowdy attempted to stand and made it, and when he had a look around, memory returned with a rush. He was still in the clump of trees, and he could see the mud-hole where the surrey had been bogged down. But the surrey was gone, and so was the man who'd been levering it out of the mud, and the other, that still-faced fellow who'd been aboard the train and who'd buffaloed Rowdy as neatly as Rowdy, a short while before that episode, had buffaloed Stonehead Jackson. And of course the two who'd been inside the surrey, the girl and the grey-faced man dressed in a widow's weeds, were gone, too. Rowdy groaned.

Stonehead Jackson's gun lay where it had fallen from Rowdy's hand when Thane Buckmaster had levelled him. Picking up the weapon, Rowdy said, "I had a horse . . ."

"We've got him," Stumpy said. "Found the cayuse grazing not far away."

"What fetched you here?"

"Stull took me to Latigo, Rowdy. I figgered it out that you'd turned the china hoss over to the gal on the train. Went to her hotel, but she'd moved out and left the place upside down. MacLean, here, and the sheriff showed up, and we cut for sign on her. There weren't any. But we headed out along the wagon road, thinking we might happen to pick up a clue. Great feller for clues, this sheriff. Then we almost rode on top of you. Just what's the idea of snoozin' in the middle of a road, Rowdy?"

Pickens plucked at Stumpy's elbow. "Then this is the partner you were telling me about?"

Stumpy gave Rowdy an apologetic glance. "The sheriff was itchin' so hard to arrest somebody for kidnappin' Miss Jones that I began shaping up as the likeliest candidate. I had to tell him that we're doing a special job for Clee Drummond. It shore cooled him down. Rowdy, shake hands with Sheriff Slim Pickens."

Pickens peered hard. "So you're Rowdy Dow! I've seen your picture on reward dodgers. You don't favour it much."

"Thanks," Rowdy said and extended his hand. "Now tell me this, Sheriff. Who lives hereabouts that wears a cloak dragging to his heels—a still-faced gent who came in on the afternoon train?"

"Why, that's Thane Buckmaster. Owns a place he calls the Eagle's Eyrie, a big house on up the slope of the hill."

"I like you, Sheriff," Rowdy said solemnly. "And when I like a man, I don't mind throwing a little business his way. The gent who kidnapped Miss Jones and her—er—mother is this same Thane Buckmaster. I recollect that house on the hill. Saw it when we came over Latigo Pass. We'd better be heading up that way. I'd be pleased to help you make the arrest."

Pickens's jaw sagged. "Thane Buckmaster! You must be loco! Buckmaster's the wealthiest man in the basin. Why in tarnation would he be kidnapping folks? He's a queer galoot, and there ain't any of us really knows him, even though he's been here for years. But I can't say he ever struck me as a criminal. Where did you get such a notion?"

Rowdy shrugged. "I was heading for Latigo and minding my own business. I found a fancy rig bogged down in this mud-hole. A big fellow was working at getting it out. This Buckmaster gent was standing by, watching. Inside the rig was the girl and her mother, bound and gagged. That fetched me off my horse with a gun in my hand. But I should have watched Buckmaster instead of the other fellow. That poker-faced galoot swings a mean gun."

Slim Pickens shook his head dazedly and muttered an incoherent something, and Logan MacLean faced the sheriff. "We'd better be getting up to the Eagle's Eyrie," MacLean said heatedly. "Dow didn't dream all this. Buckmaster may be a leading citizen hereabouts, but if he's holding that girl and her mother, he's going to have *me* calling on him. With or without the law behind me!"

Pickens, obviously recalling the wisdom he'd bought from the Acme people, suddenly became co-operative. "Buckmaster, eh?" he said darkly. "He's a Jekyll and Hyde, that's what he is! Come to think of it, I always did have him sized up as worth watching. He fooled a lot of people with his smooth ways, but he never fooled Slim Pickens. Come on, fellers. I'm deputising all of you. We'll have a look inside the Eagle's Eyrie."

Horses were ground-anchored nearby, and they swung astride them. The night was nearly gone, Rowdy noticed, and that meant he'd lain beside the road for a considerable time before Stumpy Grampis had stumbled upon him. Turning to Stumpy, he said, "Seen anything of Stull or his boys?"

"Left Stull on the edge of Latigo," Stumpy told him. "For all I know, he's still there. When me and the sheriff and MacLean was a few miles out of Latigo, we run into a bunch of fellers headin' towards town. From what I could see, I pegged 'em for Stull's crew. But the way they was burnin' leather, they didn't have time for a look at me. Likely they figgered we was three cowpokes headin' home after a night in town. How did you skin out of the school-house, and what put Stull's boys in such a lather?''

The four were riding in single file with Slim Pickens up ahead and Logan MacLean close behind him, and Rowdy and his partner had dropped far enough to the rear to be able to hold a private conversation. Whereupon Rowdy explained how he had put suspicion into the minds of Stull's men and sent them in search of their leader, and then told about the smoke-filled bottle that had fooled Stonehead Jackson. Stumpy chuckled, but sobered with a new thought.

"Destiny's shore dealing us queer cards," he opined. "We start out by helping a badge-toter, Clee Drummond, who's laid his marshal's badge aside. Now, danged if we ain't deputy sheriffs! That's gonna be hard to live down, Rowdy. But I reckon I know what's in your head. That gal's got the china hoss, so you're stringin' along with the law to help git the gal, and git the cayuse. It's all part of the same chore.''

"There's more to it than that, Stumpy. You guessed right about what became of the cayuse. When Stull came aboard the train, I told him I didn't have the horse, but I was only bluffing. It was in my hat. Then I got it to the girl. But to-night, I only told that lawdog up ahead what he needed to know. Mrs. Jones has got a moustache, feller. What do you make of that?''

"You mean she's a man?''

Rowdy nodded. "A man I've seen somewhere—sometime. But darned if I can place him.''

"Could be anybody," Stumpy decided. "You've covered a heap of territory in your time. So that black dress was just a disguise, eh?''

"That's right," said Rowdy.

Dawn was greying the eastern sky when they came past the schoolhouse, and Rowdy and his partner exchanged glances when they saw only one horse at the hitchrail. Yet by the very nature of things, Bat Stull and his crew would shortly be returning here after a fruitless quest in Latigo for the elusive Stumpy Grampis. Rowdy breathed easier when the schoolhouse had fallen behind them as the trail tilted upward toward the summit of this mighty hill. The appearance of Bat Stull at this time would have constituted a nuisance.

Climbing was slow, arduous work; the new day made the going a little easier, but Rowdy was tired enough to start nodding in his saddle. His head still throbbed, and he tried remembering when last he'd had a genuine night's sleep. He concentrated on trying to recall landmarks from the trip down this same trail the day before, but the trees bore a fraternal similarity, and he was quite surprised when Slim Pickens turned off the trail, and Rowdy, lifting his eyes, saw the high outlines of Thane Buckmaster's house through the screening timber. Pickens reined to a halt.

"Me and Dow will go on," he said. "You fellows wait here, out of sight. If Buckmaster's turned to kidnapping, he's a desperate man. If me and Dow don't show back in half an hour, say, you two head for Latigo and fetch a posse up here."

Patently Logan MacLean would have preferred being one of those who stormed yon darkling fortress, but the railroad man apparently saw the wisdom of Pickens's strategy, for he made no protest. The sheriff had risen in Rowdy's estimation by this piece of sagacity, and Rowdy said, "That's straight thinking, mister. An ace-in-the-hole will make me happier when we climbs into that spider web."

Thus it was decided, and with Stumpy and MacLean left behind, Rowdy and the sheriff rode on through the timber. Buckmaster's place, it developed, consisted of a barn and corrals and other buildings, as well as the house, but it was the big structure that held Rowdy's eyes. Two-storeyed, it had a number of gables, and it was painted a shadowy green that made it one with its surroundings. Rowdy hadn't cottoned to this house when he'd seen it yesterday; now, faced with the prospect of entering it on dangerous business, he was even less enthusiastic. But when Pickens slid from his saddle before the long gallery and mounted the steps, Rowdy was at his side. An eerie silence held the place; the ranch, if such it was, hadn't awakened to the new day, and when Pickens lifted a heavy iron knocker on a ponderous door, its clangour echoed thunderously.

Silence. The knocker clanged again, and something stirred

furtively within the depth of the house. Then the door opened, and Curly Bill Callaghan stood peering at them. The foreman was fully dressed, and Rowdy instantly recognised him as the man who'd been prying the surrey from the mud-hole a few hours before. Pickens said, "Buckmaster in, Callaghan?"

"I reckon," Callaghan said. "Step inside."

Coming into a hallway that was like a dark tunnel, they were left standing. Doors gave off this hallway, and Callaghan had vanished through one of these, and now he reappeared, beckoning to the visitors. They stepped into a high-ceilinged room, grey and uninviting at this hour, and here they found Buckmaster awaiting them, a sombre figure against a background of carved furniture and an opulence that was colourless. Buckmaster, too, was clothed, and he said, in his clipped, precise way, "Good morning, Sheriff. What brings you out so early?"

"I ain't looking for worms," Picken said and unleathered his gun, a move so unexpected that Curly Bill Callaghan, standing just within the doorway, was too late to match it. "You're under arrest, Buckmaster," the sheriff went on. "I'm hoping you'll come peaceful. *Easy, Callaghan!* I'm watching you!"

Callaghan's right arm uncrooked, and Buckmaster frowned. "What in blazes are you talking about?" Buckmaster demanded.

"Kidnapping is the charge," Pickens said. "You snatched a Mrs. Jones and her daughter from the Empire last night. I reckon you fetched 'em here. Trot 'em out."

The ghost of a smile crossed Buckmaster's graven face. "Bill, will you see if Miss Jones is up?" he said. "If she is, ask her to step down here."

Callaghan obediently bobbed from the room, and Rowdy instantly stiffened, sensing a ruse on Buckmaster's part to get Callaghan out of the room. How, when and where Callaghan would appear again was a matter for conjecture, but Rowdy was suddenly glad that Stumpy and Logan MacLean had been left posted outside. A few silent minutes chased each other into eternity, and then, to Rowdy's utter astonishment, Callaghan came into the room again. And with him was Miss Jones, a robe pulled over her nightgown, and her hair hanging to her waist. She looked at Rowdy and recognised him; Rowdy was sure of that. But before she could speak, Thane Buckmaster said, "These gentlemen are labouring under some sort of delusion. Will you explain that you and your mother are my guests."

"*Guests!*" Slim Pickens blurted.

"Certainly," Buckmaster said. "I saw them on the train, and I saw them alight at Latigo. I'd meant to speak to them, but I got into an argument with John Crenshaw, who was waiting for me at the depot. After I'd started for home, it came to me that it would be a hospitable gesture to offer them this place to stay while they were in the basin. So I went to the Empire and looked them up, reasoning that they'd be at the only hotel. They were gracious enough to accept my invitation. Isn't that right, Miss Jones?"

The girl nodded woodenly.

"Now look here!" Pickens said with some heat. "I saw the hotel room they had. It was turned upside down. All the sign read that they'd been taken from it by force."

Miss Jones said, "The room was in good order when we left it to go with Mr. Buckmaster. But the clerk wasn't at his desk, so we couldn't check out. Mr. Buckmaster said he'd have his foreman ride into town to-day and explain to the hotel management. If our room was upset it must have been done by someone who came there after we'd left. Possibly some hotel prowler found the door unlocked and decided to search for valuables."

Rowdy spoke up now. "Look, miss," he said. "I saw you in Buckmaster's rig last night. You were bound and gagged."

Buckmaster glanced at Rowdy with new interest. "I've been wondering where I'd seen you before," Buckmaster said. "You boarded the train at Jubilee, didn't you? And you were removed by holdup men later. And last night you came along as my foreman was extricating my surrey from the mud. Sorry about that clout I gave you. But you gave us quite a turn. You took one look at us and piled off your horse, a gun in your hand. My instant presumption was that you were a holdup man."

"Then you admit I *did* see you on the road, and that you buffaloed me?"

"Of course. But there's certainly no sense to your story that Miss Jones and her mother were bound and gagged in my surrey at that time. They were in the rig, certainly. It was quite muddy underfoot, and I didn't ask them to alight."

Slim Pickens's brow was pleated. Once again he'd run into something that wasn't covered by any of the lessons he'd so far received from the Acme people. "Just what is this, Dow?" he demanded. "It all adds up, but it doesn't give the right answer. The girl ought to know whether she was kidnapped or not."

"Of course I should," Miss Jones said. "I can't explain our dishevelled hotel room. As I've said, that must have happened after we left. But I certainly know that I came here of my own volition. And I don't appreciate the fact that Mr. Buckmaster is apparently under suspicion merely because he was hospitable enough to offer us quarters far more comfortable than the hotel's."

Rowdy grinned. "O.K., Miss. I know what I saw, and it was ropes and gags. Now will you call your *mother* downstairs and let us hear what *she* has to say?"

"My mother is still sleeping," Miss Jones said emphatically. "And I don't propose to disturb her. You tried making a nuisance of yourself on the train, Mr. Whatever-your-name-is. Now you persist in making a nuisance of yourself again. Please go away."

"Look," said Rowdy heatedly, "I dropped a little china stallion in your lap aboard the train. I'd like to get it back. Or are you going to tell me that that was all a dream, too?"

"I have the stallion," Miss Jones said, and dug a hand into the pocket of her robe. "Here it is."

Thane Buckmaster said, "If the thing is this man's property, I suggest you give it to him, Miss Jones. He seems to be—er—a little eccentric. It's probably best to humour him."

"If you think I'm loco——!" Rowdy blazed, but Slim Pickens's hand was upon his arm. The girl crossed to Rowdy and pressed the china stallion into his palm. She said, "We got in very late last night because of getting bogged down. If you'll excuse me, I'll finish my sleep."

Slim Pickens said, "We'd better go, Rowdy. Seems there's been a mistake somewhere."

Rowdy looked down at the china figurine in his hand. At least he'd succeeded in getting it back, but there was none of the elation in this moment that there might have been.

Not when events had taken the turn they had. For, just as surely as porcupines had quills, either Miss Jones had cleared Thane Buckmaster by a string of lies, or Rowdy Dow had had an optical illusion the night before. And, considering how forceful the girl had been in her contention, Rowdy was even beginning to doubt himself.

9. Some Cards Are Faced

ROWDY DOW CAME DOWN the trail from the Eagle's Eyrie talking to himself, and he wasn't sure he could trust the answers he got out of his muttered monologue. For Rowdy was beginning to suspect that he wasn't exactly a sound person. Twice, lately, he'd been batted over the head with a gun-barrel. Clee Drummond had laid a forty-five over Rowdy's skull in a Jubilee saloon, and Thane Buckmaster had likewise pistol-whipped him beside the road leading into Latigo, last night. Maybe the continued use of the cranium as an auction block tended to scramble a man's brains. Maybe, from here on out, he'd be seeing cows climb trees and rabbits chasing dogs. Hadn't he already seen a man and a girl bound and gagged and held prisoner and then later talked to that same girl only to be told that she was the grateful guest of the one who'd been responsible for the ropes and the bandannas?

Rowdy shook his head. The four were in single file again, Slim Pickens up front and Logan MacLean trailing behind the sheriff. Stumpy Grampis was next in line, and Rowdy brought up the rear. When they dropped down to the schoolhouse, that one horse that had been at the hitchrail was gone. There were no school children in sight, nor any sign of activity. According to Rowdy's calculations, this was a week day, and he put a shouted question to Slim Pickens for verification.

"School kids are all in town to-day," Pickens shouted back. "Getting booths set up for the county fair which will be starting soon. Makes a nice holiday for the kids."

Now here was information a man could grab hold of. Kids still went to school on week days, and they still welcomed a chance to get away from their desks. Obviously some things hadn't changed. The sun still rose in the east, and would likely set in the west. Winter followed autumn, and it would probably snow one of these days. Rowdy felt considerably heartened.

Onto flatter land, Rowdy moved up beside Stumpy and said, "We told you all that happened inside the house. What do you make of it?"

Stumpy wrinkled his leathery face. "That hotel room looked like a Piute camping ground. Whether it got messed up before or after the Joneses moved out, we can't prove. But the sheriff saw it too, and so did MacLean. That's why the sheriff's up ahead there, shaking his brains till they rattle. He's plumb puzzled, Pickens is. Look, Rowdy: you *sure* the Joneses was tied up in that rig?"

"Sure as shooting."

Stumpy gnawed at his down-tilted moustache. "When I found that gal missing in Latigo, I made me a guess that her disappearance had something to do with the china hoss. In other words, I figgered she'd been grabbed because she had the stallion. But she turned it over to you with no argument, and Buckmaster let her do it. *That's* the thing that don't make sense to me."

"But neither the girl nor Buckmaster knows how much that horse is worth."

"They know it's worth enough that Bat Stull come aboard a train and took you off in order to get it," Stumpy said.

Rowdy fell silent. There was nothing to be gained but a headache by any further discussion of the subject, and at least he had the china stallion once again. That made his next move clear, and when they were well along the wagon road winding toward Latigo, Rowdy jogged to a position beside Pickens. "I've got to see a man named John Crenshaw," Rowdy said. "Where do I head from here?"

"Crenshaw? He might be in Latigo at his bank, or he might be out at his ranch this morning. If you cut overland, you can't miss the spread." Pickens waved a thin arm in a general westerly direction and proceeded to enumerate landmarks. Logan MacLean, an exceedingly glum young man since they'd put the Eagle's Eyrie behind them, now quickened with interest. "That's odd," he remarked. "I've got business with that same John Crenshaw. Mind if I ride along?"

Rowdy shrugged. "Why not?"

And so they parted from Slim Pickens, that bewildered lawman continuing along the road toward Latigo while the three headed for the distant ranch of John Crenshaw. The sun climbed toward zenith, and Rowdy alternately dozed in his saddle and gazed at the expanse of Latigo Basin, having his first real look at this lush and tawny land. A cow could keep contented here, he judged, unless it was the kind that worried about its waistline. There was plenty of feed and plenty of water, and hills to shelter beef herds from the winter blizzards. Good cows, when they died, doubtless went to a place very much like Latigo Basin.

Rowdy had taken a third hitch at his belt and was wondering, by the time they reached Crenshaw's, if grass was likewise good for humans to eat. The ranch buildings were many and well-kept, though far from opulent in appearance, and when they dismounted before the ranch-yard gate, Crenshaw appeared on the gallery, and Rowdy, accosting the big, red-faced man, learned his identity and was impressed. For this man's sake, Clee Drummond had persuaded Butch Rafferty to an act of atonement, and Rowdy's instant judgment was that John Crenshaw was worth it. Crenshaw likewise gave Rowdy a long, calculating look as they shook hands.

"Rowdy Dow, eh?" said the banker-rancher. "I've seen your picture. You don't look much like it. But come inside and have a bite to eat, all of you. Likely you've ridden a long ways."

Rowdy tried not to hurry too fast, and, seated at a table, he also managed to wait until the food was passed to him before heaping his plate. While the three were eating, Rowdy said, "Clee Drummond sent me to you. I'm to meet him here. I take it he hasn't showed up yet. I've got an article to deliver to him, or to you, if he doesn't get here inside a week."

Crenshaw's bushy eyebrows bunched. "Drummond and I are old friends. I've had quite a bit of correspondence with him these last few months. If you're working for him, likely you know what it's been about. Drummond's had the notion he can recover some loot that Butch Rafferty, the outlaw, stole from me years ago. I don't mind saying that it's mighty important to me—and to a lot of other folks—that I get that money back. I hope you bring good news, Dow."

"That money is likely as good as in the bank," Rowdy said. "Pass those fried spuds this way again, will you, Stumpy?"

Logan MacLean shoved back his plate. "My business here is as agent for the railroad, Mr. Crenshaw," he said. "There are two things my company wants in Latigo Basin. And we're told that you're the man who can solve both our problems."

Rowdy looked longingly at an uncut apple pie upon the table and then reluctantly said, "If this is private, me and Stumpy can go outside."

"No need," MacLean assured them with a grin. "The point is, Mr. Crenshaw, that the railroad is building a spur through to join our main line farther north. That's no secret. But we'll want right-of-way through Latigo Basin. That means that we're prepared to pay certain ranchers considerable sums for the privilege of laying our rails across their lands. We're told that you usually handle the business dealings of the ranchers."

Crenshaw's eyes widened; in them was astonishment, a fleeting hope, and then a smouldering anger. "So the railroad's building through Latigo," he said hoarsely. "Now I'm beginning to savvy something that was a mystery to me. I'm afraid you'll likely have to do your dickering with a party named Thane Buckmaster. He'll shortly control most of the basin. Up until now I couldn't understand why he wanted the ranchers under his thumb. Railroad right-of-way usually sells high."

"Buckmaster!" Logan MacLean was obviously beginning to grasp a truth, too. "The man with the cape. He was in our division headquarters office a few months ago, just about the time it first became public that we were considering a spur. I saw him there. Then I saw him again on the train into Latigo yesterday. Yes, I can just about assure you that Mr. Buckmaster knew we had our eye on Latigo Basin."

Crenshaw began pacing, and Rowdy forgot his interest in food in watching the man, for here he saw a genuine regret and a genuine concern that were completely unselfish.

Crenshaw was a man who had suddenly awakened to the truth of why his neighbours were shortly to be swindled. Little as Rowdy understood about the situation, he could understand that. And now he saw why Clee Drummond had been so desperately anxious to help this John Crenshaw, and the significance of the china stallion became more apparent. Crenshaw was bucking Thane Buckmaster, and money was the sinews of their kind of war.

Crenshaw, looking at MacLean, said, "I don't mean to bother you with my own troubles. What was the other piece of business that fetched you?"

"A need for beef. Our grading crews will be head-quartering at Latigo shortly, then pushing up through the basin. We'll have to feed those men. The best way will be to buy beef on the hoof from the local ranchers. Do you suppose they can pool their herds and get us a thousand head, say, to Latigo within the next few days? We'll pay spot cash at the Eastern market price."

Crenshaw ceased pacing as abruptly as though he'd walked into a wall. "*Cash for beef?*" he ejaculated, a new light in his eyes. "Man, do you realise what you've just offered this basin? Salvation!"

"I'm afraid I don't understand," MacLean said.

"Look. Folks have had a bad year, hereabouts. The Eastern market price dropped just enough that by the time the ranchers paid freight to Chicago or Omaha, they'd be taking a loss on their critters. More than that, last winter was a hard one, and some had to import feed. That left everybody short of working capital. My bank wasn't strong enough to stake them, so a group pooled together and borrowed money from Thane Buckmaster. In place of collateral, he got six-months options on their places—the idea being that if they didn't repay the money, it would be considered as Buckmaster's down payment on the ranches at prices set in the option. That blanket option will be up in another thirty days or so. Do you see Buckmaster's scheme? He'd learned that the railroad would come in here, buying right-of-way. And by the time that happened, he expected to be the owner of the very ranches the railroad would want. And he stood a fair chance of winning, too. Folks haven't even started fall roundups this year. No sense in gathering cattle to sell at a loss. But now you've changed the picture.

Eastern prices paid at Latigo means they'll be able to realise a profit. Mister, inside an hour every man of my crew will be riding to spread the word that beef's to be gathered and headed for town!"

MacLean came to a stand. "Then I'll be getting back to Latigo, Mr. Crenshaw. I'll see you later."

"You bet you'll see me," Crenshaw said exultantly. "When your company turns over the money for the cattle, I'll either be buying that option from Buckmaster or handing out the money to the ranchers to do the same thing. And when you want to negotiate for right-of-way, you'll be doing your dickering with the real owners, the men who have sweated to build this basin."

MacLean nodded at Rowdy and his partner. "Pleased to have met you gents," he said. "I've got to admit that I'm more concerned than ever over the Jones girl. This Buckmaster seems to be a sinister sort."

"Some cards have been faced," Rowdy conceded. "But don't worry. The last hand hasn't been played."

MacLean gone, Rowdy said, "Thanks for the grub, Crenshaw. I could use a place to bunk. Haven't slept since I was fourteen, seems like. Will you wake me if Clee Drummond shows up?"

Crenshaw said, "You bet. The bunkhouse is out back. My crew's gone mending fence. I'll have to ride after them and get them started carrying the word to the other ranchers. Dow, you don't know what this means to me. I'm ten years younger for having talked to Logan MacLean."

"And me, I'm getting older every minute I go without shut-eye," Rowdy said. "So long."

But when Rowdy and his partner had found their way to the bunkhouse and stretched themselves out, Stumpy staved off sleep long enough to say, "What do you make of it all, Rowdy?"

"It's shaping up," Rowdy observed drowsily. "I like this Crenshaw gent. He sets a good table. But I'm in this for Butch Rafferty. You remember, I told Drummond I owed Rafferty a favour. Butch wanted that hundred thousand dollars restored to Crenshaw, or Rafferty wouldn't have told Clee Drummond where the marshal could lay his hands on the china stallion. And Crenshaw needs the money to buck Thane Buckmaster's scheme. Maybe that railroad beef deal will change everything. But my chore is to turn the stallion over to Drummond.''

"I keep thinking of that pore little girl up there in that buzzard's roost on the hill,'' Stumpy said. "You reckon we should pay another visit to the Eagle's Eyrie?''

But Rowdy was already asleep, and it was a long and dreamless sleep that lasted until deep darkness had fallen. He awakened to find the bunkhouse silent except for the lusty snoring of Stumpy, and he judged that Crenshaw's crew was still gone on the mission to the other ranchers. Stamping into his boots, Rowdy shook his partner.

"Maybe we missed the call to supper,'' Rowdy said. "But I sure aim to find out.''

Coming out of the bunkhouse, they groped across the ranch-yard to the lighted house, and Stumpy said, "You reckon it might take Drummond a spell to get here? I could enjoy resting.''

Rowdy, about to make a reply, never voiced his comment, for at that precise moment he almost stumbled over an object. They had rounded the house, and at this point they could see the light splashing from a big bay window to lay a saffron rectangle across the gallery and upon the yard, but here the shadows were thick. Bending, Rowdy found a man sprawled upon the ground, a man who had apparently been approaching the ranch-house but hadn't quite reached it.

"Who is he?'' Stumpy asked.

Rowdy got a match aglow and had a look. "Clee Drummond!'' he ejaculated, and the match burned down to his fingers unheeded. For Drummond's face was crusted with blood, and he had the look of a man who'd gone two fast rounds with a buzz saw and lost the decision.

Rowdy scraped another match aglow. "Give me a hand with him, Stumpy,'' he said.

Drummond opened his eyes then and regarded the pair of them blankly, and Rowdy said, "Easy, feller. We'll be taking care of you. Who messed you up like this?''

He wasn't sure whether Drummond understood, and it took the marshal a mighty effort to speak. "Rafferty!'' Clee Drummond gasped. "Butch Rafferty . . .'' And then his voice trailed off to nothing.

10. Dead End Trail

BETWEEN THEM THEY CAME carrying Clee Drummond up the gallery steps, and when Rowdy kicked lustily at the door, John Crenshaw opened it, had one look and hastily led the way to a bedroom. With Drummond stretched upon the bed and a lamp aglow, the three made a quick examination of the man, Rowdy explaining the while how he'd found the marshal sprawled in the yard. Drummond, it developed, had been grazed along the head by a bullet and had lost blood. His clothes were considerably dishevelled, but otherwise he appeared to be unhurt. He'd lapsed into a deep unconsciousness, but his heart was steady and his pulse regular.

Rowdy, his lips drawn tight, said, "I suppose the nearest doctor is in Latigo. Come on, Stumpy. We'll be riding."

Crenshaw said, "I'll bathe his wound, meanwhile, and bandage him the best I can. My crew hasn't returned yet, so there's nobody to go but you boys. Ask for Doc Pettibone when you reach town."

Whereupon Rowdy and his partner, without further ado, borrowed the two speediest-looking saddlers to be found in Crenshaw's corral, laid gear onto them with considerable alacrity, and hit the trail. Rowdy had an idea as to the general direction of Latigo, and he cut straight overland, pushing the horse as hard as he dared, and Stumpy managed to keep abreast of him. It wasn't until they paused to blow their horses that they had any chance at talking, and Stumpy said then, "How do you figger it now, Rowdy? Don't make sense that Clee Drummond got hisself dusted by Butch Rafferty. First place, Rafferty was friendly enough with Drummond to give the marshal the secret of the china stallion when Drummond got the idea of restoring stolen loot

73

to John Crenshaw. Besides, Rafferty is still in Deer Lodge Pen.''

"We can't go too much on what Drummond said when we found him there in the yard," Rowdy observed. "I asked him who messed him up. He said, 'Butch Rafferty.' But maybe he didn't even hear my question. The point is that he started me thinking, Stumpy. Now I'm remembering where I saw the man who was bound and gagged in Thane Buckmaster's fancy rig—the man who came to Latigo wearing a woman's dress. It was Butch Rafferty, amigo.''

Stumpy nearly fell off his horse. "*Butch Rafferty!* Escaped from the pen?''

"They didn't pin a rose on him and turn him loose.''

Stumpy was thoughtfully silent. Then: "I didn't know you knew Butch Rafferty's face when you ran into it. Shucks, Rowdy, you couldn't have been much more than a button when Butch got sent away to Deer Lodge.''

"It's a long story," Rowdy said. "It starts years back when my Maw and Paw had a two-bit place up in the Little Rockies, and I was knee-high to the pump handle. That was before Rafferty organised his Wild Bunch; he was lone-wolfing it then. He hit our place one night and came tearing in and asked for a quick change of horses. A posse was on his heels, savvy. Paw knew him, and the old man would have been willing to help, but Paw had troubles of his own that night. You see, Maw was mighty sick—so sick that Paw didn't dare leave her to go fetch a doctor from town. And I was too little for a chore that size.''

Stumpy said, "You know, Rowdy, I'd never ever stopped to think that you once had a Paw and a Maw. It don't seem natural.''

"Paw explained things to Rafferty," Rowdy went on. "And Rafferty stayed at the ranch while Paw headed to town for a sawbones. You understand me, Stumpy? Rafferty sat there for a matter of hours, wringing out cloths and laying them on Maw's forehead, one ear cocked all the time for the sound of the posse that might be cutting sign on him. Rafferty helped a lot of folks in his time. He strewed around the money he stole, and that's why there was a regular relay of ranches where he could get help—places like the one in Latigo Basin where he later left one hundred thousand dollars. But what Rafferty gave the Dows that night was

more than money—he risked a chance at capture to help a
two-bit rancher who was in a tight.''

"Some things," Stumpy said slowly, "are beginning to
make sense to me now.''

"Rafferty got away on one of our horses, but the posse
showed up shortly after Paw got back with the sawbones.
And Paw was jailed for aiding and abetting Rafferty. He
went to the pen, and that broke Maw's heart, and she died.
Growing up as a jailbird's son wasn't easy, and that's what
started me on the owlhoot, old horse. Paw died in Deer
Lodge Pen. But none of that changes the fact that Butch
Rafferty did something for the Dows that I can't shake out
of my head. When Clee Drummond asked me for help in
Jubilee, I didn't take the chore for Drummond's sake. You
know that. I took it because I owed a favour to Butch
Rafferty.''

"And you remembered Rafferty's face from that night
when you was a button?''

"Some boys grow up wanting to wear a tin badge. Me,
I wanted to get big enough to join Rafferty's Wild Bunch.
I followed them in the newspapers, and I've still got the
clipping, somewhere, that tells about Butch being captured
and tried. Yes, I remembered his face, but he's older now,
and I didn't get much of a look at him last night. The girl
must be Myra Rafferty, his daughter. The papers mentioned
her at the time of his trial, but she was only a kid, then.
Come on, Stumpy. To-night it's my turn to be the one who
is riding for a sawbones. The sooner Clee Drummond is
patched up, the sooner we'll find out what he meant when
he mentioned Butch Rafferty's name.''

They jogged their horses into action again, and there was
no more talk between them as the miles unreeled. The lights
of Latigo were soon visible, but it was late evening when
they approached the town. Along a railroad siding lay a
string of freight cars, and, on a flat stretch of prairie nearby
and at the western outskirts of town, lanterns bobbed and
tents had mushroomed and many figures moved busily.
Stumpy looked at this spectacle in considerable amazement
until Rowdy guessed the truth. "Folks getting the county fair
set up," Rowdy judged. "You remember, the sheriff
mentioned it.''

Stumpy pointed a wavering finger. "Don't know how

many blue ribbons they'll be passing out, but the gent that fetched in yonder turnip is certainly a cinch for a prize. *Jumpin' Jehosophat!*"

"That," said Rowdy, "is no turnip. It's an ascension balloon, part of the show, I reckon. They've probably just unloaded it and they've inflated it to-night to make sure it's in working order."

"An ascension balloon," Stumpy marvelled. "What's the world comin' to? The next thing you know, it won't be safe for a bird to go flying alone."

"We've got a sawbones to find," Rowdy reminded him.

Into the environs of the town, they asked the location of Doc Pettibone and were directed to a cottage on the other side of Latigo. Riding down the main street, Rowdy was suddenly mindful that Bat Stull and his crew might be about, but that was a risk that had to be taken. They found Pettibone's cottage swathed in darkness, but, after diligent pounding upon the door, Pettibone appeared, a rotund, fussy little man, with a pair of trousers pulled on over a nightgown.

"You trying to smash the door off the hinges?" he demanded with a scowl.

"Gunshot case needing your attention out at Crenshaw's ranch, Doc," Rowdy explained. "Get your black bag and come along."

"Gunshot case!" Pettibone snorted. "Always gunshot cases. And in the middle of the night, too. Never could understand it. A gun can be fired twenty-four hours of the day, but fellows always pick midnight to get themselves shot. They must think a doctor doesn't have to sleep!"

He bobbed back into the house, leaving Rowdy and his partner waiting on the porch, and in due time Pettibone appeared again, fully clothed and bearing his black bag. He led the way to a small shed behind the cottage and quickly saddled a horse and swung to its back.

"Or take a banquet," he muttered morosely. "Never got past the soup at any banquet without some inconsiderate fool getting shot just about that time and needing attention. Why do people always get messed up at meal time? They must think a doctor doesn't have to eat!"

The medico between them, Rowdy and Stumpy came again along the main street, and this time Rowdy gave a glance to John Crenshaw's bank, a solid-looking structure which stood almost directly across from the courthouse. When they skirted the fair grounds, the doctor was deep in a new tirade against humanity in general and people who were so thoughtless as to stop bullets in particular, and Rowdy suddenly laid his quirt along the flanks of the medico's horse. "Time's a-burning, Doc!" Rowdy shouted. "Got to get loping."

Crenshaw's ranch-house was aglow with light when they reached it, and there were lights in the bunkhouse, too, and several loop-legged individuals in the yard, so Rowdy judged that at least part of Crenshaw's crew had returned. Crenshaw was pacing his living-room when Rowdy prodded the doctor inside, and Sheriff Slim Pickens was also here, sprawled in a chair.

"Drummond's conscious now," Crenshaw reported. "I did the best I could for him, but he'll likely need some stitches. Go on into the bedroom, Doc. Dow, you and Grampis look done in. Have you met Sheriff Pickens? He dropped by to pass the time of day and decided to stay until the doctor arrived."

"We've met," said Rowdy. "When do we get to see Drummond?"

"Soon as Pettibone says it's O.K."

The doctor eventually put in an appearance, rolling down his sleeves and shrugging into his coat. "A bad flesh wound," he said. "But rest will fix him up. He's asking for Rowdy Dow. Ten dollars, please."

Crenshaw produced money, and Rowdy plucked at the banker-rancher's elbow. "Come on," Rowdy said. "We might as well all go in."

Clee Drummond sat propped against pillows, his head bandage-swathed and the colour gone from his face. But his heavy-lidded eyes were alert enough, and he managed a wan smile. Rowdy said, "We're all hankering to know just what happened to you."

"Bat Stull and his bunch cornered me in the livery stable over in Jubilee yesterday," Drummond said. "Or was it day before yesterday? They combed me pretty fine for the china stallion. Naturally they didn't find it."

"I know," Rowdy said. "I've seen Stull since. But that's

another story, and it will keep. When did you head for Latigo?''

"That same afternoon. I was all ready to start when the Jubilee town marshal got a telegram. Seems that Butch Rafferty had managed to get over the prison wall. He's been in the prison hospital for some little ailment or other, but he started shamming once he was well, and he fooled the guards into getting careless. The telegram was to warn the law to be on the lookout for him. Butch didn't leave much sign, but it all pointed to this end of the state.''

"You mentioned Rafferty's name when we picked you up out in the yard.''

"I'm getting to that. I came to the top of Latigo Pass easy enough, but it started raining and deep dark caught up with me, and it was slow going after that. About halfway down this side, I saw the lights of a house through the trees. It was long after midnight, as near as I could judge, and I figured I'd beg a little hospitality and put up for the night. So I headed toward those lights.''

Slim Pickens, propped against the wall just within the doorway, stiffened. "The Eagle's Eyrie!'' he ejaculated.

"A surrey had just pulled into the yard, or so I gathered,'' Drummond went on. "The horses were still hitched to it, and two men had dismounted. One held a lighted lantern and was helping two people from the back seat of the rig. Those people were tied and gagged, and one of them was Butch Rafferty's daughter Myra, and the other was Butch himself. Damned if he wasn't wearing a dress, but I know him. It would have been a mighty big surprise if I hadn't seen that telegram in Jubilee and known he was on the loose, and it took the wind out of me as it was. And just about that time, I was spotted.''

Rowdy shot a meaning glance at Slim Pickens. "Guests of the house!'' Rowdy said scathingly.

"The fellow with the lantern was cutting the ropes that tied the two prisoners,'' Drummond went on. "The other, a fellow in a long cape, was holding a gun on them. Rafferty's gag had just been removed, and Rafferty looked my way, and I'll swear he recognised me. Anyway, he shouted, 'Help me!' But the fellow with the gun had spied me, too, and he let loose with it. The bullet opened my scalp, and that's the last I remember of that night.''

"Thane Buckmaster," said Rowdy, "has a habit of using a gun first and asking questions later. Sooner or later, it's going to get him into trouble. Sooner, I reckon."

Drummond raised a hand to his bandage. "When I came to, I was stretched out in an upstairs bedroom. That must have been sometime to-day. It was a long drop to the ground, but they'd made the mistake of leaving bedding, and I fashioned a rope. Got down and into the timber and looked for a chance to help myself to a horse, but the sign never shaped up right. So I lit out on foot. It was a mighty long day, and this head wound started bleeding again, and I remember fainting quite a few times. But I made it."

Rowdy said, "The way it adds up, Slim Pickens and me were in the house at the very time you were unconscious upstairs. But at least I know why you had Butch Rafferty on your mind when we found you here. Now why in blazes is Thane Buckmaster holding Rafferty prisoner? And why is Rafferty's girl stringing along with Buckmaster?"

"One hundred thousand iron men is your answer," Stumpy opined. "Rafferty, in person, is just as valuable as the china stallion. Buckmaster's got wind of that lost loot."

Slim Pickens said, "I got a wire to-day about Rafferty. The net is being spread for him. And Thane Buckmaster has really over-stepped himself. Either he's a kidnapper, or he's sheltering a fugitive, or both. I'll be seeing him pronto. There'll be quite a feather in the Stetson of the gent who returns a famous galoot like Butch Rafferty to Deer Lodge Pen."

Rowdy dug into a pocket and produced a tiny china figurine and held it so that Drummond could see it. "Here's your horse," he said.

Drummond looked at the china stallion for a long moment, and the bleakness left his face. "I didn't trust you completely in Jubilee, Rowdy," he said. "That's why I wouldn't say how valuable that horse really is. You see, I wasn't sure but what you might go after a certain treasure on your lonesome. But Stumpy made mention of one hundred thousand dollars. You know?"

"Stull talked. He wanted us to throw in with him. I know everything but the name of the rancher who'll surrender the money when he sees the horse. It wouldn't have made any difference. I don't want my pardon revoked."

Drummond looked up at John Crenshaw. "I told you in my letters that I had a notion I could recover the money that was stolen from you years ago. I guessed that Butch Rafferty might want to make restitution once I told him about you and your bank, and I was right. Your troubles are about over, John. I think I can put that hundred thousand in your vault mighty soon. And when you're counting it out, remember that you owe it to three men who have never been very friendly with the law—Butch Rafferty, Rowdy Dow, and Stumpy Grampis."

Crenshaw's bushy brows came together. "But what about Rafferty? What moved him to make an escape right now, and what fetched him straight to Latigo Basin? Did he change his mind about restoring that money? Maybe he's after it himself."

"If you knew Butch Rafferty, you wouldn't think so, John. He's an old man, and he was mighty willing to string along with me." Drummond shook his head. "Why he escaped remains to be seen. I'm mighty sorry he did. I have some influence with the governor. Once that loot was restored, I intended going to the governor with the whole story. It probably would have meant a pardon for Rafferty. But he had to go over the wall!"

Crenshaw said, "I can certainly use that money, Clee. A fellow from the railroad came to-day with a proposition that will beat a scheme of Thane Buckmaster's to swindle the basin, but there are slips between the cup and the lip. One hundred thousand dollars in my vault, and we've won."

"Then tell me," said Drummond, "where we'll find a basin rancher named Sam Usher."

"Sam Usher——?"

"Usher is the man who buried that loot for Butch Rafferty years ago. And Usher is pledged to surrender it to the man who fetches him the china stallion that Rowdy has in his hand. I can give my pledge to Usher that the law will never bother him for having held that loot all these years." Drummond glanced up at Slim Pickens. "Sheriff, I reckon I can count on you to back me up in that."

"So Sam Usher buried that money for Rafferty," John Crenshaw said dazedly.

And suddenly, then, the room was silent, and in that breathless moment John Crenshaw turned older; the elation that had been in his eyes was gone, and his shoulders were stooped. "Sam Usher," he said in that same dazed voice, "is gone. He moved out of the basin years ago. Practically disappeared overnight. Come to think of it, he left just about the time Rafferty was captured and put on trial."

Rowdy sighed explosively. "That was the one flaw. I told Bat Stull as much. The man who had that loot was bound to run off with it once Rafferty was behind bars. Stull didn't think anybody would risk double-crossing Rafferty while the old gent was still alive. So Usher's gone." He looked at the stallion in his hand, then thrust it back into his pocket, a worthless object.

"I remember Usher," Slim Pickens said. "Feller from the East. He wasn't here long. Came out and took up a little land, but he never made much of a go of it. I'm not surprised that he was running one of those relay stations that Butch Rafferty used to have."

"He hailed from Ohio," Crenshaw said tonelessly. "I remember he came into the bank once for a loan and mentioned something about his old home town."

"Ohio?" Slim Pickens murmured. "Is that anywhere near Cleveland? Me, I'm a student of the Acme School of Detecting and Criminology in Cleveland."

Crenshaw's eyes lighted with hope. "A man like Usher with a hundred thousand dollars would head back to his old home town to let folks know how well he'd done in the West," Crenshaw decided. "Wire those detective people of yours, Slim. Ask them to check at Ashland, Ohio, on a Sam Usher who once lived there. Give them a complete description of him. You remember. He was a tall, skinny fellow with a wild tangle of hair, and he always needed a shave."

"I'll wire 'em to-night," Pickens promised.

Rowdy ran his sleeve across his forehead. "This," he said, "calls for a walk in the fresh air. Stumpy, my head's aching again. We deliver the stallion and call the job quits, and it turns out that the man who's waiting for the horse has disappeared. And there goes the thousand dollars that Drummond hoped to pay us."

But once out onto the gallery, Rowdy sloughed off all signs of dejection. "Snake out a fresh pair of cayuses, Stumpy," he said quickly. "We're riding. To the Eagle's Eyrie. And we've got to get there before the sheriff fetches a posse up the hill. Pickens wants Butch Rafferty in order to send him back to Deer Lodge. Me, I'm seeing that that doesn't happen. I wouldn't risk my pardon for Sam Usher's buried loot, but I'll risk it for Butch Rafferty's freedom. This is where an old debt gets paid off.''

11. Lady Luck

THE HOUR THAT BAT STULL had spent on the outskirts of Latigo the night before, impatiently awaiting the return of Stumpy Grampis who had presumably gone to awaken the postmaster, was the longest in Stull's dubious career. True, the hour consisted of the usual sixty minutes, and each in turn had the customary sixty seconds. This, Stull learned, after some laborious cogitation, added up to three thousand, six hundred seconds. Considering that he was going to get his hands on a very tidy sum by virtue of this waiting, he tried to divide one hundred thousand dollars by three thousand, six hundred seconds in order to determine the amount earned in each second, but he found himself bogged down in a maze of arithmetic that made his head ring. And still there was no Stumpy Grampis.

An hour was an hour, no matter how you chopped it up, and Stull began sweating at its end. Should he go into Latigo and have a look around? There was that business of having boarded a train over on the other side of the hump, and the remembrance of his own temerity had made Stull as nervous as a bare-footed man in a blizzard. Also, there was the fact that he'd accosted Clee Drummond in the Jubilee livery stable and forcibly searched the marshal. Ordinarily a great fellow for playing safe, Bat Stull had been too dazzled by the prospects of one hundred thousand easy dollars to be careful of late. All of which could mean that the law might be looking for him. Latigo, therefore, had little allure. And so he pondered, balancing avarice against fear but never quite tipping the scale, and while the minutes chased each other into oblivion, five men came roaring out of the north, lashing their horses as though they were trying to outrun their own shadows. Stull, recognising them, raised his voice in a surprised shout.

"What in blazes fetched you boys here?" he demanded as they sawed hard on the reins.

These were his own men, and suddenly they were a speechless lot. They had come frantically across the miles, spurred by the suspicion that Rowdy Dow had adroitly planted within them; they had come hoping to find Bat Stull here, and yet not sure but what Stull had gotten the china stallion and gone to collect the long hidden loot. Stull's very presence, proof that they had been mistaken in suspecting a double cross, locked their jaws. Stull said, "Talk up! Where's Stonehead Jackson? And what about Dow? Don't tell me he slipped away from you!"

One said sheepishly, "Jackson's watching Dow."

"Then why in thunder——?"

Luke, he of the low hairline and the blunt manner of speech, said, "You might as well know it, Bat. We got thinking maybe you wouldn't be coming back with that dinero. It crossed our minds that you'd been careful never to tell us the name of the rancher who's gonna turn over that money once he sees the china hoss."

"It wasn't any secret," Stull said angrily. "Not from you boys. I got the whole story from Stonehead Jackson. You know that. And I left Jackson with you. He could have told you that a gent named Sam Usher hid Butch Rafferty's money years back."

"Where's Grampis?"

"That's what I'm wondering. He's been gone over an hour now. Something tells me he won't be coming back."

"Maybe," said Luke, "you was too cocksure that Grampis would turn over the stallion to save Dow's hide. Supposing Grampis is lone-wolfing it? Likely he's burning leather to Sam Usher's place. With the stallion."

"Seems to me," another spoke up, "that we've been tackling this job all wrong. Why chase around after the stallion? Let's head out to Sam Usher's right now. If Grampis has gone there, we'll be on hand to take the money away from him. If he hasn't, maybe we can persuade Usher to give us the money—without the stallion."

There had been times when Bat Stull had toyed with this very idea. He had even considered various ways by which

Sam Usher might be more readily persuaded to surrender Rafferty's loot. Most of them had been mighty rough. But that cautious streak in Stull had argued that it was better to get his hands on the stallion and present it to Usher. The stallion represented a pledge made by Sam Usher to Butch Rafferty, and the stallion would turn the trick with a minimum of effort and risk. But the stallion had turned into a sort of pint-sized Pegasus and gone winging. For a long moment Stull contemplated the various phases of the situation, and then he said, "You boys are right. We'll go straight to Usher. But first a couple of us will have to head into town and find out just where Usher's place is located. Luke, come along."

Jerking his sombrero low, Stull led the way. He was still not enraptured over the idea of entering Latigo, but circumstances left him little choice, for, whatever fear a man might hide in his heart, he had to display boldness to those who followed his lead. And so Stull and Luke came riding boldly along the main street, and in this manner they came upon that inexhaustible mine of information, the Oldest Citizen.

Each town has such an antique fixture, and Latigo was no exception. A mixed blessing, the Oldest Citizen was the living proof that Latigo's was a healthful location, but he was also the repository of much ancient scandal, the man who remembered things better forgotten, the skeleton in everyone's closet. To-night this favourite child of Father Time hunkered on the edge of a boardwalk, diligently whittling as he watched the lights blink out in such saloons as were already closing. Stull, sighting him, reined to a stop and, deciding upon an air of friendly condescension as the best approach, said, "Howdy, Dad. Pretty late for you to be up, isn't it?"

The ancient instantly bristled. "Don't need as much sleep as you'd think," he snapped. "Don't go burnin' the candle at both ends, the way you young uns do."

"Pretty well acquainted around here?"

"That depends," was the cryptic reply.

"Know where we can find Sam Usher's place?"

"Yup. Follow the wagon road north, but turn left where it forks to climb up toward Latigo Pass. Go about eight miles farther north and you'll hit the place. Can't miss it."

"What sort of galoot is this Sam Usher?"

The Oldest Citizen shut his jackknife. "A no good galoot. Bachelor fellow. Comes from a good family back East, but you'd shore never know it. Never shaves. Never takes a bath. Friend of yours?"

Stull ignored the question. "Thanks, Dad," he said. "Reckon we'll find the place all right."

"Won't do you no good," said the ancient.

"Why not?"

"Sam ain't there. Ain't been there for ten years. Moved away."

"Jumping Jehosophat!" Stull ejaculated. "Why didn't you say so in the first place?"

"You didn't ask. You just wanted to know where his place was. It's still there. Follow the wagon road north, but turn left where it forks and——"

But Stull had already nudged his horse and was riding away, the silent Luke following after him. And so they came again to the outskirts of the town and to the men who awaited them there, came to report that they'd followed a dead end trail all these miles. It made a black night blacker. Every one of these men had spent his cut of that hundred thousand dollars a score of times in fancy. There was some swearing.

"There's just one piece of satisfaction to be got out of this," Stull said vehemently, when all else had been said. "I want to see Rowdy Dow's face when I tell him that that blasted china stallion isn't worth a plugged peso!"

But that little pleasure was denied Stull. With his men trailing along, he came back toward the school house, and somewhere ahead of them this night were Stumpy Grampis, Logan MacLean, and Sheriff Slim Pickens, riding in the hope of cutting sign on the kidnappers of the missing Miss Jones. Had Stull's crew stayed on the wagon road, they would have come to the place where Stumpy found an unconscious Rowdy Dow beside a mud hole, but the bunch chose instead to head directly overland, skirting the dark, pine-clad hills and heading for the schoolhouse as the crow flies. They'd have been wiser to emulate the owl on a night like this. When the moon set, they became hopelessly lost, and it was dawn before they reached the schoolhouse and saw that only one horse remained at the hitchrail.

Stonehead Jackson had recovered from the blow Rowdy

Dow had been forced to strike. Again the giant was hunkered behind a desk, and again he was diligently reading the *Arabian Nights*. He looked very much as Stull's men had last seen him, except that he had not thought to remove the dunce cap which Rowdy had placed on his head.

"Where's Dow?" Stull demanded as they came trooping in.

The giant looked up from the book. "Gone," he said.

"Gone! Where? How did he get away?"

"I'm busy," said Jackson and turned back to his laborious reading.

Stull began pacing an aisle. "To blazes with Dow," he decided at last. "Let him chase after the stallion, if that's what he's doing. He'll find out sooner or later that Sam Usher left the basin. Come to think of it, he had a hunch that the rancher who buried Rafferty's money might have dug it up a long time ago and hit the grit with it. But if he really believed that, why was he messing around with the stallion."

"We'd better get out of here," one of the men said. "The kids will be coming to school in a few more hours."

"Me, I'm takin' a look at Usher's place," Luke declared. "Ain't much of a chance that Usher left that dinero behind when he quit the basin, but I want to make sure that old coot in Latigo was telling it straight about Usher leaving."

Stull's crew had become a rudderless lot, lacking any new goal to replace the old one toward which they had steered so futilely. Now a new hope gave them incentive to move again, and they headed outside and began piling into saddles. Stull didn't urge Stonehead Jackson to come. The giant's usefulness had ended when he'd told the story of what he'd overheard between Clee Drummond and Butch Rafferty in the prison hospital, and now Jackson stood as a living reminder of a dream that had been blasted. But Jackson tucked the book into his shirt front and followed along. The wagon road brought the group back into the basin, and eventually they found the fork that led northward. The sun was well above the rim of the hills when they reached Usher's former home.

It was no place for a picnic. There was a one-room shack, musty with desertion and littered with the debris of hasty departure, a tumbledown corral, and a barn of sorts that tilted crazily. An examination of the premises revealed nothing more valuable than a rusted kettle and a battered tin plate, and these Stull savagely kicked aside while a squirrel taunted him from the single, stunted tree which grew within the yard. But at least there was solid planking in the floor of the shack, and Stull said, "This will be better than spreading our blankets on the ground. Me, I could use some sleep."

Stonehead Jackson had begun one of those freakish monologues he sometimes uttered. Anyone who listened carefully would have thus learned about the genie in the bottle, and all the details of how Rowdy Dow had tricked the giant, but no one was interested. The outfit bedded down and slept away most of the daylight hours, and they awakened to find Lady Luck still frowning upon them. An examination of all the saddlebags revealed that in calculating the durability of their food supply they had forgotten to consider the inroads made by the voracious appetites of Stumpy Grampis and Rowdy Dow. A sparrow couldn't have lasted a day on what was left. Stull looked at the lowering sun and said, "We might as well be getting out of Latigo Basin. We'll do our eating when we get over the hump to Jubilee."

Piling into saddles again, they returned to the trail that tilted downward from Latigo Pass, and they began the ascent, a sullen, silent lot. Night overtook them while they were still far from the summit, and they grew more sullen with the full realisation that they shouldn't have attempted this climb at such a late hour. But there was nothing to do but forge onward, and they single-filed in continued silence until they saw the lights of the Eagle's Eyrie shimmering through the trees. Luke, the rebel, drew to a sudden stop. "I'm heading over there and asking for a bite of supper," he said emphatically. "To blazes with the risk. Whoever perches up here on the slope wouldn't have us on a wanted list."

Stull, too, was hungry enough to be beyond argument, and he nodded. Wending through the trees, they came to the great, shadowy house, and Stull, self-appointed spokesman, dismounted and climbed to the gallery and hoisted the knocker. Thane Buckmaster, himself, came to the door, and Stull said, "Sorry to be bothering you. We seem to be half-way to nowhere. Would we crowd your cook-shack?"

Thane Buckmaster gave him a long and intent look. "I remember you!" he said then. "You're the man who came aboard the train yesterday and took those fellows off at the water tank. You had a bandanna over your face, but I'm sure it was you."

Stull took a quick step backward, his hand falling instinctively toward his holster, but Buckmaster smiled. It was the first time Buckmaster had smiled since Curly Bill Callaghan, gone riding down into the basin, had returned an hour before with a piece of news. The news had been that John Crenshaw's riders were hurrying to certain ranchers with word that cattle were to be rounded up for delivery to Latigo for the railroad's construction crew.

"Easy, man," Buckmaster said. "I'm not the law, you know. Come inside, and fetch your crew along. I think I could talk business with a fellow of your daring. Are you interested?"

Interested? Stull smiled, too. He had already measured the signs of opulence in Buckmaster's establishment and in Buckmaster's garb, and strong in Stull was the feeling that his luck had finally changed. Maybe this trip to Latigo Basin wasn't going to be fruitless after all.

12. Rowdy to the Rescue

IT WAS MUCH LATER that same night when Rowdy Dow and Stumpy Grampis came riding across Latigo Basin, their destination the Eagle's Eyrie. They came astride a pair of borrowed Crenshaw saddlers, and Stumpy, denuded of armament since first he'd fallen into Bat Stull's hands, had also helped himself to a six-shooter he'd found in Crenshaw's bunkhouse. Rowdy still wore Stonehead Jackson's gun, and that made the two of them fashionably dressed for their purpose—the freeing of Butch Rafferty from Buckmaster. Yet Rowdy rode with no planned strategy. He was aware of the maxim that although there were more ways to kill a cat than choking it to death with buttermilk, it was first necessary to catch the cat. He covered the miles with no other thought than to reach Buckmaster's place.

The new day was dawning when they left a pair of jaded cayuses behind them and came easing through the timber toward the big house. Rowdy was glad now that he'd sawed his share of wood in Crenshaw's bunkhouse the previous afternoon; a man might dislocate his jaw if he did too much yawning, and, besides, he needed to be awake if he were to best Buckmaster. When he and Stumpy had screened themselves behind bushes in such a position as to command a view of both the house and the barn, the door of the latter structure slid back and a man emerged and headed toward the cook-shack. Stumpy stared, sucked in a long breath and said, "Bat Stull! Now we find him *here*. It's a small world."

"Getting downright stuffy, if you ask me," Rowdy said.

Other familiar figures put in appearances, and large among them was Stonehead Jackson. "The whole crew's moved in," Stumpy observed. "Do you suppose they've gone to work for Buckmaster? That don't sound like Bat Stull, though. He likes easy dollars.''

"Maybe," Rowdy mused, "Bat has learned what we learned—that Sam Usher hit the grit. That left Bat footloose and fancy free. Now he's tied up with Buckmaster. Birds of a feather, old horse.''

"Look!" Stumpy ejaculated. "Rafferty's gal has just come out of the house.''

Sure enough, Myra Rafferty had stepped down from the gallery of the great, gloomy pile, and she came wandering aimlessly across the yards. She was as sweet-faced as ever, Rowdy noticed as he watched her progress, but about her there was a dark and haunted look. Then he held his breath as she drew nearer to where he and Stumpy were hidden. And that was when Rowdy's plan was born, and, to his partner's utter astonishment, Rowdy whistled softly. The girl raised her head, her blue eyes questing the concealing bushes, and Rowdy whispered, "Miss Rafferty! Over here!''

He hardly knew what reaction to expect, and therein lay the gamble. The previous morning this girl had insisted that she was Thane Buckmaster's guest, and Rowdy had found no way of shaking her story. But since then he had learned that she was Butch Rafferty's daughter, and that had provided a great deal of food for thought. Thorough mental mastication had failed to make the puzzle less puzzling, but at least Myra Rafferty didn't scream and flee now. Coming closer, she said softly, "Who's there?''

"Me. Rowdy Dow. Can you leave the yard, or are you being watched from the house?''

"I don't think so," she said and wormed her way through the bushes to where they crouched. "I've been hoping you'd come back," she said breathlessly. "I should have recognised you yesterday, of course. But I didn't begin to understand until the sheriff called you Rowdy. I've heard of Rowdy Dow. But you don't look much like your picture.''

"We're here to help. You weren't telling it straight when you claimed I was mistaken about seeing you and your dad bound and gagged in Buckmaster's rig. How come?''

"You saw what you saw, of course. After we'd put up at the Empire House the day we arrived in Latigo, Thane Buckmaster and his foreman came to our room. When the train had stopped at that water tank on the other side of the hills, it stopped so abruptly that Dad's hat and veil were jarred off. I recovered the hat quickly, but it seems that Dad was noticed. By Thane Buckmaster.''

"I was snoozing at the time," Rowdy confessed. "The jar woke me up.''

"In Latigo Buckmaster told us he was taking us to his house. Dad put up a fight, and that's how the room got turned upside down. We didn't dare yell for help. That might have fetched the law, and we didn't want the law. You see, Dad had gone over Deer Lodge's wall.''

"I know. You helped Butch escape from stony lonesome?"

"Yes and no," she said. "Dad smuggled a letter to me by means of a convict who was being released. In the letter Dad said that he intended to make a play at escaping on a certain night. There was no way I could safely get word back to him, begging him not to try anything so foolish. It was either ignore him or help him, so I chose to go to Deer Lodge on the night he'd mentioned. Since I couldn't stop him from escaping, my best bet was to make sure that his escape was successful. It was my idea to disguise him as a widow, and I fetched the proper clothing with me.''

"And then you came to Latigo. And Buckmaster recognised your dad on the train. That's easy to understand. Butch took a better picture than I did, and his picture was in all the papers at the time of his trial. But what in blazes did Buckmaster want with Butch Rafferty?''

The girl shrugged. "He's never told us. After he fetched us here, he was worried because he'd met you on the road. And then he had to use his gun on another man, a fellow who rode into the yard just as we reached the house that night. Dad tells me that that man was Clee Drummond, the federal marshal. Once we were fetched into the house, Buckmaster told me I'd better insist we were guests if anybody came asking questions. Otherwise Dad would be exposed and dragged back to Deer Lodge. That's why I talked as I did to you and the sheriff. Supposing I'd told the truth? The sheriff would have arrested Buckmaster, but he'd also have arrested Dad. Since then we've been comparatively free, though Dad isn't allowed to leave the house. And Buckmaster is sure that I won't run away. He'll turn Dad over to the law if I do.''

She glanced imploringly at Rowdy. "You said you were here to help. Please do. I know a great deal about you, and I'm trusting you. The papers said you were something of a Robin Hood when you were an outlaw."

"There was a difference," Rowdy said drily. "Usually I robbed the rich and kept it for myself. But I aim to help Butch Rafferty, and I think I know how. Stumpy, you keep the lady company. And if I don't show back, I want you to load her on my horse and get her to Crenshaw's ranch. Got that straight?"

Whereupon Rowdy came to a stand, extricated himself from the bushes and headed boldly toward Thane Buckmaster's house. Stumpy called frantically after him, but Rowdy paid no heed. He came across the yard unchallenged, and, climbing the gallery, he opened the door and strode purposefully down the hall and into that same high-ceilinged room where he'd been summoned the previous morning. Nothing had changed. Thane Buckmaster was here, and so was Curly Bill Callaghan, and they both came to their feet in astonishment as Rowdy put his back to the doorway and folded his arms. Buckmaster said, "*You!* What's the meaning of bursting in here like this?"

"I've come," said Rowdy, "to take Butch Rafferty off your hands."

"Butch Rafferty? What in blazes are you talking about?"

"Maybe you're still calling him Mrs. Jones," Rowdy said. "Look, Buckmaster, we'll both save time if you quit bluffing. I know Rafferty's here. So does Clee Drummond. Or have you forgotten about Drummond? The man you clipped with a bullet out in your yard the other night. You were mighty frisky with that gun for one evening, mister!"

Callaghan took a belligerent step forward, but a gesture of Buckmaster's stayed the foreman. "Drummond?" Buckmaster echoed. "The federal marshal?"

Rowdy shrugged wearily. "Now don't go telling me I'm dreaming again. After Drummond got away from this house, he made it to John Crenshaw's ranch. I was there, and so was Sheriff Pickens when Drummond told his story. Do you know what that means? Pickens will be here sometime today to relieve you of your house guests, mister. Maybe you can talk yourself out of that. But it might be better if you didn't have Rafferty around. You might be jugged for aiding and abetting his escape. Tell me this, Buckmaster. What was the idea of fetching Rafferty out here?''

Thane Buckmaster smiled. ''I saw Rafferty's face on the train. I didn't recognise him then, but I got to wondering why a man was disguised as a woman. After I'd reached Latigo and started for home, it came to me who he was. I'd seen his picture, of course. I got an idea then. Money is my business, mister, and I keep an eye out for an easy dollar. Obviously there'd be a reward posted for Rafferty. Instead of turning him over to that dolt, Pickens, I intended holding Rafferty here until a reward was offered.''

''A flea wouldn't choke on all the water that story will hold,'' Rowdy commented. ''But it doesn't much matter what you *really* had up your sleeve. I'm here to keep Rafferty from being grabbed by the law. So take your choice. Turn him over to me, or hang onto him and let Pickens find him here. Which will it be?''

Buckmaster sagged into a great leather chair and began drumming his fingertips upon the armrest, his eyes narrowed with thought. This was, Rowdy reflected, like a poker game without cards; there was the same business of pitting your hand against the other fellow's and bluffing when there was nothing else to do. Hope flared in Buckmaster's eyes, and the man said, ''Supposing I stick to my story that I invited the 'Joneses' here as my guests? Supposing I keep on insisting that I clouted you because I thought you were a holdup man? And how was I to know Drummond was Drummond? He came at me with a gun in his hand, too. And supposing I tell Pickens that only this morning did I discover that 'Mrs. Jones' was a man? And to prove that I'm law-abiding I'll have only to surrender Rafferty to Pickens.''

Rowdy shaped up a cigarette and took a thoughtful drag on it. ''It won't do, old son,'' he said. ''You've forgotten Myra Rafferty. She's on our side, and my partner's got her hidden out in the timber right now. And she can make a liar out of you because she can tell everything that happened from the moment you showed up in the Empire in Latigo. But if her daddy rides away with me, Myra rides along with us, which means she won't be talking to Pickens. That's why you'll be smart to give me Butch Rafferty.''

Buckmaster lifted his gaze to Rowdy. ''What's *your* game?'' he asked pointedly.

"Me?" said Rowdy. "I'm the biggest damn' fool that ever climbed over Latigo Pass. I've told you my game: to keep Rafferty from going back to stony lonesome."

Buckmaster came to a stand again. "You win," he said. "The girl makes all the difference." He glanced at the sullen Curly Bill. "Fetch the old man down here."

"We'll need a couple of horses for the Raffertys," Rowdy said when Callaghan had departed. "Likewise a sack of grub to keep us while we're holed up in the hills. That's part of the bargain, too."

And then Curly Bill Callaghan was stepping back into the room, and with him was a stocky man, seamed of face and grey with prison's pallor, a man with a porcupine haircut and a heavy moustache. He had discarded a widow's weeds for Levis, a shirt, boots, sombrero and a jumper, and, although these clothes had obviously been Callaghan's and were too big, the stocky man wore them with a certain dignity. And it was Rowdy's thought that this was a moment that required a roll of drums and a fanfare of high, brassy music; and the years rolled back for him, for again he was standing in the presence of the greatest owlhooter of them all, the man who'd become a legend, Butch Rafferty.

Rafferty said, "What's this about me being turned loose?"

"This man is taking you and your girl with him," Buckmaster said.

"The law will be here pronto with a posse," Rowdy explained. "I'm Rowdy Dow. Likely you don't remember me. I owe you a favour from away back. I aim to have you deep into tall timber when that posse shows up. There's no time now for talk. Will you come along?"

Rafferty gave him a steady look, and there was puzzlement in the oldster's eyes at first, and then a sort of fatalistic acceptance of the fall of the cards. "I'm ready," he said.

And so it was that Rowdy Dow emerged from the Eagle's Eyrie with Butch Rafferty at his side, and when Rowdy gestured toward the bushes that screened Stumpy and Myra Rafferty, the two hesitantly showed themselves. "It's all right," Rowdy called. Turning to Thane Buckmaster who stood on the gallery, he said, "Get those horses, and don't forget that sack of grub. Have Bat Stulls do the saddling. I want to see his face when he finds me here."

Buckmaster's eyebrows lifted. "You've seen my crew?"

"Too often lately," said Rowdy. "Hurry, now."

Ten minutes later the three men and the girl were astride horses and heading through the timber away from the Eagle's Eyrie, Butch Rafferty upon a leggy piebald and his daughter upon a grey. And Thane Buckmaster stood on the broad gallery and watched until they'd faded from sight. Then Buckmaster turned to Curly Bill Callaghan who waited silently at his side.

"I allow myself one mistake a year, Bill," Buckmaster said. "I think I made one when I let myself be stampeded into snatching Butch Rafferty from the Empire House. But to-day's doings rectified that. It's Mr. Rowdy Dow who'll now be sought by the law for aiding and abetting an escaped convict. But Dow knows that Stull is here. That might spoil the little plan I had in mind when I hired Stull's outfit last night. Have Stull and his men get out of sight before Pickens shows up here. In fact, it might be best if none of us were at home when the sheriff arrives."

"And after I send the crew away, boss——?" Callaghan queried.

"Follow Dow and his outfit," Buckmaster said. "We can make Sheriff Pickens believe anything as long as Rafferty or his girl or Dow and his partner can't contradict us. There's only one sure way to make certain that none of them will ever talk. I'm leaving that up to you, Bill."

"I reckon," said Callaghan, without smiling, "I understand."

13. Hideout in the Hills

ROWDY RODE AWAY FROM the Eagle's Eyrie with a feeling that he was being followed, and it wasn't the persistence with which his own shadow kept up with him that tolled that warning bell. In the old days, such a feeling would have meant that there was a lawman on his back trail. To-day he reasoned that if riders were cutting for his sign, those riders likely drew Thane Buckmaster's pay. More than that, he was troubled by the thought that he'd somehow played into Buckmaster's hands by the little coup that had freed Butch Rafferty from the Eyrie. Yet Rowdy had seen only one way to accomplish his mission, and it had worked.

He kept his fears to himself. They were single-filing along with Rowdy in the lead, the two Raffertys strung behind, and Stumpy bringing up the rear, and such a formation precluded talking. When they came to the trail that tilted downward into Latigo Basin, Rowdy crossed it and led his little cavalcade into the timber beyond. Pine grew thick here and the going was slow. But at last he found a game trail that crawled along the shoulder of the hill, and, within an hour, he came to a creek that brawled down into the basin. Forcing his mount out into the icy waters, Rowdy headed the cayuse upstream, the others stringing along behind him. When Rowdy elected to climb to the far bank, Butch Rafferty proved that he understood such strategy and saw the need for it.

"You folks ride on a piece," Rafferty said. "I'm an Injun when it comes to covering sign. They'll never find the spot where we left the creek."

Rowdy nodded. In some circles Rowdy might cut considerable swath as a purveyor of owlhoot lore, but he knew that compared to Butch Rafferty he was a novice. When Rafferty overtook them a half-hour later, the veteran outlaw was grinning bleakly and the clay of the creek bank was on his knees. Rowdy knew then that the hoofprints had been obliterated.

But still Rowdy was not content, and he took to circling and back-tracking, but always he climbed higher on the hill. In this manner they came to where the timber was thinner and here scattered shale, although it offered treacherous footing, left little sign of their passage. And then they found the cave.

It was tucked back into the hillside, and it had a scattering of boulders around its entrance that effectively screened it from casual eyes. Obviously it had been fashioned by the gods of the lawless as a sanctuary, and three pairs of eyes lighted as they inventoried its merits. Even Myra caught the instant excitement of the men, but she frowned as Rowdy stepped down from his saddle.

"You're not thinking of staying *here?*" she queried.

"It isn't much—but it's home," Rowdy announced. "At least for a few days. Possemen are going to be thicker than fleas on a sheepdog in these hills. There's no use trying to get over the hump until they get tired of chasing their own shadows."

Rafferty said, "He's right, Myra. We've got to hole-up for a spell. Unless you want your old dad to be caught and hauled back to stony lonesome."

Rowdy had his own ideas about Butch Rafferty's future, but this was not the moment to air them. The horses hobbled and stripped, the saddle blankets and other gear were carried inside the cave which proved to be high-ceilinged enough to allow Rowdy, the tallest of the group, comfortable passage. They delved into the grub sack Buckmaster had provided, and they ate cold food, not yet daring a fire. The afternoon was long, and Rowdy spent most of it stretched upon his saddle blanket and sleeping intermittently. When evening came, Rafferty said, "I've gathered some smokeless makings, and I've done some scouting. If anybody followed us from that big house, we shook them off hours ago. I'm going to take the chill out of the air."

There is something about a fire that draws men closer, that brings their shoulders to touching and their souls as well.

True, it wasn't much of a fire that Butch Rafferty built; as fires went it was definitely in the yearling class, but it wrought the customary magic. Myra smiled wanly in its feeble light, and, looking at Rowdy, she said, "This is the first real chance I've had to thank you for what you've done."

Her father said, "And this is the first real chance we've had for talking. I remember you from the train, Dow. You dropped a little china hoss into my girl's lap—a hoss I hadn't seen for a good many years. From the talk between you and that big galoot that had come aboard to take the hoss away from you, I gathered that you was packin' that hoss for Clee Drummond. Right?"

Rowdy nodded. "That's shore finished, I reckon. But I'm still paying off an old debt. And there are things I've got to know. We're all tied together now, for better or for worse, as the sky-pilots put it. Rafferty, I'd like to hear why you busted out of Deer Lodge."

The old outlaw sighed. "I spent ten years there. I'd have been satisfied, I guess, to put in the rest of my life behind those walls. And then Clee Drummond came to see me and everything changed."

Again Rowdy nodded. "Drummond talked you into letting him know what you'd done with one hundred thousand dollars you'd stolen from John Crenshaw."

"That's right," Rafferty said. "I always hit the big boys when I was owlhooting—the banks and railroads and express companies. Drummond showed me where I'd made a mistake when I picked on Crenshaw. He told me a heap about Crenshaw and how the feller had built a bank from scratch, and he told me how that robbery had just about ruined Crenshaw. Also, he explained that Crenshaw needed that money mighty bad right now—to save a bunch of Latigo ranchers from getting themselves swindled by a sneaking money-lender who was out to get his hooks into all the basin. By the time Drummond finished his spiel, I saw that I hadn't robbed just one big man when I'd lifted that money. I'd robbed a lot of little fellers. That's why I told Drummond the story of the china stallion and let him know where he could get hold of that little hoss."

"But it must have been just about then that you decided to escape."

Rafferty's face hardened. "Drummond told me a few other things," he said. "They didn't mean much at the time, but when I got around to thinking about them and putting them together, I realised that Drummond had been letting me know just how the law came to dab a loop on me years back. I was sold out, Dow—double-crossed. And if I got Drummond's hints for what they meant, the Judas who put the law on my trail was a certain Sam Usher—the same gent who buried that hundred thousand dollars for me somewhere in the basin!"

Rowdy sucked in his breath. "You mean that Drummond, knowing that Sam Usher was the one who put the sign on you, still figured Usher had left the money buried and would be willing to turn it over to him?"

"Drummond was taking that chance," Rafferty said. "But let me tell you about Usher, and maybe you'll understand. I never knew Usher very well. He had a shoestring outfit in Latigo Basin, and I rode in one night and laid gold on his table and told him I'd like to be able to pick up a horse and grub in a hurry if the need ever arose. I had a string of such relay stations stretching plumb to Mexico in those days. Usher was willing to do business. He wasn't much of a specimen, but two things struck me about him—he was greedy, and he was patient. Also he was some impressed by me; I had a wide rep then. Maybe Drummond figgered the same as I'm figgerin'—that Usher, after double-crossing me and landing me in the pen, has been biding his time. Ten years, twenty years . . . what's that against one hundred thousand dollars? When I die, he figgers to dig up the money. Meanwhile, he plays it safe. Don't you savvy? Any show of wealth on his part might reach my ears. And that would prove to me that if he hadn't double-crossed me to the law, at least he'd double-crossed me by helping himself to my loot. With me alive, Sam Usher wouldn't risk that!"

"And so you jumped the pen to look for Sam Usher!"

Rafferty's eyes grew frosty. "Usher will hand that money back to me," he said. "And I've got to see that the dinero gets returned to John Crenshaw. After that, I'll look at Sam Usher through gunsmoke. Maybe I've had these years in Deer Lodge coming to me, but I didn't have them coming from Sam Usher. When I've done those chores, I'll go back to the pen."

Rowdy shook his head. "Why not go back now? Clee Drummond thinks he might be able to get the governor to pardon you. You've jeopardised that by escaping, but maybe it isn't too late. It will be if Sam Usher's blood gets on your hands."

Rafferty said, "I've got to get Sam Usher."

Rowdy sighed. "I'd hoped I could talk you out of it without telling you the truth. If you'd changed your mind about Usher, this wouldn't be bad news for you. But here it is: Sam Usher left these parts years ago. Right after your trial. Any fool can see that the hundred thousand likely went with him."

Rafferty came to a stand, and he was magnificent and terrible at this moment. He said, "You think I'm a stubborn old hellion who has to have another man's scalp because of a double-cross that's ten years old. You think I'm forgetting this girl who's got an outlaw and a jail-bird for a father and who'll see me turned into a killer before this string is played out. There's more to it than that, Dow. Clee Drummond gave me a chance to do something decent to make up for all the other things I've grown old enough to be ashamed of. Now you say that Sam Usher's gone. Then Usher has spoiled my one chance to make it up to John Crenshaw and to Latigo Basin for what I did when I lifted that money. That's why I've still got to find Usher. No matter where he's gone."

Rowdy, too, arose. He said, "Try to savvy this, Butch: I'm stringing along with you. Whatever trail you're taking, I'm taking likewise, and I reckon Stumpy will tag along. Like I said in the beginning, we're in this together. For better or worse."

The frost went out of Rafferty's eyes, and he smiled an old man's smile. "You said you owed me a favour, Dow. Darned if I can remember what it might be for. But I'm beholden. Remember that. We'd better turn in for the night."

And so ended their first day at the cave, but there was another day, and another—long, quiet, do-nothing days, an idyllic existence except that there was no future in it. The nights were increasingly chillier, and it rained all of one of them, and the grub ran low. And Rowdy, at first content to sleep and to bask in the sunshine of Myra's gratitude, became impatient with a curiosity as to what might be transpiring in the basin. They had seen no signs of a posse, but whether this attested to their thoroughness in covering their tracks, or whether the law was otherwise occupied, they couldn't know. It was Stumpy's discontent that finally broke the deadlock of their hideout existence.

"Ain't enough bacon left to grease a boot toe," Stumpy complained the third evening. "Next thing you know, we'll be hunting jack-rabbits, and my ears will grow long from living on such fare. Me, I'm going down into the basin and forage for eatin' grub."

"Go ahead," Rowdy agreed. "But keep yourself scarce. Tell you what, go to Crenshaw's ranch and get the sack filled. You know the lay of the land there, and stealing ought to be easy. If you get caught, tell Clee Drummond the whole truth. He's still not wearing a badge, and maybe he's beholden enough to me for packing that china stallion—even if it was worthless—to close his eyes to what we're doing."

Stumpy departed an hour after deep darkness fell. There was no point in awaiting him, for it would doubtless be dawn before he returned. The three wrapped themselves in blankets, pillowed their heads upon saddles, and went to sleep. But Rowdy roused many times during the night, and always he strained his ears for sounds of Stumpy's return, even though a calculation of time and distance still indicated that his expectations were based on no logic. But Stumpy came before the expected hour after all, charging into the cave before sunrise and shaking Rowdy frantically.

"Got the grub?" Rowdy asked sleepily.

"Out of Crenshaw's cook-shack," Stumpy said. "Also, I got a change of saddlers. You see, Crenshaw's cook sleeps light, and he keeps a cannon under his pillow that would blow a hole through a horse at a mile and a half range. When I was fetched to Crenshaw, Drummond was still there. He's up and around now, and I talked to him fast. He hardly listened to me. That basin bunch has got new worries. That's why I split the breeze comin' back. To fetch you the news."

The Raffertys were sitting up in their blankets now. Rowdy said, "Spill it."

"You know the ranchers have been pooling their cattle for delivery to the railroad. Those basin boys made a round-up in record time, and they had all the beef gathered and ready for the trail to town. But that beef's been run off, Rowdy!''

"Run off? Rustled——?''

Stumpy nodded. ''They only left a couple of cowpokes to hold the gather. That was last night. The county fair's still going outside Latigo, and most of the boys wanted a fast ride into town and a fling at the sights. And once the main bunch had left, riders swooped down and run off the herd.''

"Anybody got an idea who they were?''

"They was strangers to the basin boys that was holding the herd. But their description made sense to Clee Drummond. Bat Stull and his boys! But there's no proving it.''

"The basin bunch cutting sign on the herd?''

"It rained last night, remember. Stull waited till it was really pelting before hitting at the herd. The tracks were all washed out. And there's a hundred places in the hills where a herd might be hid. Logan MacLean, the railroad jigger, is sympathetic, but he's got to have a beef herd pronto, and he's got to give his superiors results, not excuses. Looks like the basin ranchers won't be able to fill that order.''

Rowdy sandpapered his chin with his fingers. ''Now I'm savvying why Thane Buckmaster hired Stull's bunch. A rustling job! That beef, delivered to Latigo, would have put money in the ranchers' pockets—enough, likely, so they could have lifted that blanket option Buckmaster holds. Buckmaster did himself a nice stroke of business when he had that herd rustled. What about him, anyway? Was Sheriff Pickens up to see him?''

"He was,'' said Stumpy. ''And that means more bad news. For us. I've saved the best till the last. Drummond told me that Pickens started for the Eyrie, but the sheriff met Buckmaster coming along the road toward town. Buckmaster claimed he was on his way to the sheriff's office. Said that he'd taken in the Joneses as guests in good faith, and then danged if he hadn't accidentally caught Mrs. Jones with her hat off and discovered she was a man. A law-abiding galoot, Buckmaster had thought that that was mighty queer business and had got set to report to the law. Then you and me, Rowdy, had come along, marched into the Eyrie with guns in our fists and taken the Joneses away with us, after telling

Buckmaster that Mrs. Jones was none other than the famous Butch Rafferty.''

"And Pickens swallowed that?''

"How could he prove it wasn't so, Rowdy?''

"What about the fact that Buckmaster laid Clee Drummond out with a bullet and locked him up in the Eyrie?''

"Another mistake, Rowdy, same as him clouting you with a gun-barrel. Buckmaster claims he thought Drummond was up to mischief when Drummond dragged a gun. Drummond knows better, and Drummond has sworn to Pickens that he saw Rafferty in the rig and recognised him as Rafferty that night when Buckmaster was unloading his guests. All of which leaves Pickens whirling around in his saddle. But there's one thing that Pickens can savvy for sure: the famous Butch Rafferty is out in these hills, and you and me are aiding and abettin' him. I'm afraid you're riding the owlhoot again, Rowdy, old hoss.''

Myra Rafferty said, "So now you're in trouble because of helping us!''

"A natural state,'' said Rowdy. "Don't let it fret you. I attract trouble like salt attracts cows.''

Stomping into his boots, he stepped from the cave, Stumpy trailing along. Rowdy, his brows knitted, said, "I don't like this. I don't like any part of it. Buckmaster's going to deal himself a wrong hand sooner or later, but meanwhile he's gathering in all the chips. A little more luck and he'll rake in the pot and own the basin. It will be too late for Slim Pickens to see the truth, then.''

"Maybe we could find that missing beef herd,'' Stumpy said hopefully.

"When half the basin is probably already hunting for it? Show our faces down there, and we'll be seeing the inside of Slim Pickens's calaboose.''

He began gathering fuel for a fire; in the frosty stillness of this high place his footfalls aroused hollow echoes. And in the midst of his search, he suddenly raised his head and stiffened to alert attention.

"Listen!'' he urged. "Did you hear them, Stumpy? Riders. Half a dozen of them, I'd say. Coming through the timber and heading this way.''

Stumpy's ear perked. "I passed Buckmaster's house on

the way up,'' he said. ''There was lights in the place and movement around the yard. Maybe I was spotted and they've took the trail.''

''Either it's Buckmaster's bunch, or it's Slim Pickens with a posse,'' Rowdy judged, and at the same time he was hurrying toward the hobbled horses. ''Get the Raffertys out here, Stumpy. We've got to hit the saddle. No matter who's coming, we're in for a chase!''

14. Hue and Cry

RUNNING WAS NO NEW experience for Rowdy. In his years of owlhooting, he'd displayed his heels on numerous occasions and had developed a remarkable proficiency at making himself scarce. But now—ironically—there was nowhere to run. Whether Slim Pickens was occupied in scouring the basin in search of the missing beef herd or whether it was the thin sheriff who was at this very moment disturbing the peace of the bitter dawn by closing in on the cave, one thing was certain. Pickens had doubtless posted men at the top of Latigo Pass several days ago as insurance against Butch Rafferty's escaping the basin. Therefore it was not the law of gravity that instantly influenced Rowdy to a decision to flee downward.

But downward meant riding into the basin. And where was sanctuary in all those tawny acres? Certainly not in Latigo town, the citadel of the law. At Crenshaw's ranch, then? Crenshaw, with the approval of Clee Drummond, had lately allowed Stumpy Grampis to leave with a sackful of food intended for owlhoot consumption. That had been because Drummond had felt a definite obligation to Rowdy Dow. But to put in an appearance at Crenshaw's with pursuit hard on their heels would be to implicate both Crenshaw and Drummond, leaving them the hard choice of either openly siding with men who were beyond the law or turning Rowdy, Stumpy and Butch Rafferty over to that same law.

No, Crenshaw's wouldn't be much of a home base in the little game of hide and seek they'd be playing. And it was high time to get started. The Raffertys had heard Rowdy's frantic order to his partner, and the pair came darting from the cave, dragging saddles and blankets. All four were instantly at the business of getting gear onto the horses, and Rowdy slung the grub-sack from his own saddlehorn. The sound of oncoming riders was nearer now, and Rowdy, swinging to his saddle without a word, led the way, nosing his mount into the timber and heading downhill, the others strung out behind him.

Instantly there was a wild yell from somewhere off in the distance; the sound of flight had carried to those others and been interpreted for what it meant. Rowdy tightened his lips and took to zig-zagging through the trees, bending low in his saddle and trusting to the horse to find comparatively sound footing. No chance now of using any of a dozen time-tested devices for shaking off pursuit or covering sign. Rowdy and his bunch lacked the necessary margin of distance to put anything fancy into effect. Their only cue was to maintain that margin and hope for luck.

So far they hadn't even glimpsed their pursuers, but those riders were clinging zealously to the trail. Rowdy could hear them hooting and hollering, and the constant crashing of horses through underbrush seemed to be all around them, an indication that the pursuers had spread out in a ragged semi-circle, a piece of strategy that was instantly apparent to Rowdy. He and his group were to be kept hemmed in until they were overtaken, and there was to be no chance to lose their followers in the deep timber. And if the fugitives came to a standstill, hoping to shake off the others by remaining silent, the pursuers had only to close the circle and trap them within it.

All of which meant that no advantage would accrue to Rowdy and his friends by remaining in the timber. And meanwhile there was always the chance that someone would be stunned by a low-sweeping branch, or that a horse might break a leg on this sloping ground. Every deadfall log was a peril; every step held its menace. Rowdy cast a glance behind. Stumpy Grampis was riding grimly, intent only upon following Rowdy's lead. Butch Rafferty on the piebald, and Myra on the grey, were also holding their own. The horses that Thane Buckmaster had provided were fleet enough.

Rowdy bobbed beneath a branch that almost wrenched his sombrero away and ceased his zig-zagging then, determined to find a game trail and head for the basin's floor. Maybe on a straight sweep of ground they could outrun the pursuit.

The sun reared itself above the eastern rim of the basin, and the chill went out of the air. Orienting himself, Rowdy veered to the south, but he'd about decided that he was lost when he finally burst upon the wagon road wending down the hillside.

They were below Buckmaster's place, but they had yet to reach the schoolhouse. Now there was nothing to obstruct their way, nothing to worry about but the steeper pitches of the trail, and Rowdy urged his mount to greater effort. They came roaring down the slant and passed the schoolhouse, not pausing to blow their horses until they reached the basin's floor. Above them reared the hill, pine-darkened and peaceful to the eye, and Rowdy, contemplating it, wondered if by luck he'd actually eluded the pursuit. The minutes trickled by, and then the riders appeared, pouring down the trail, and in their lead, his cloak bannering out behind him, was Thane Buckmaster.

That, Rowdy observed, at least settled the problem of who was pursuing them. Thane Buckmaster had five men at his back, and three of them Rowdy thought he could recognise—Bat Stull, Stonehead Jackson, and Curly Bill Callaghan. That meant that at least a couple of Stull's men were elsewhere—doubtless holding that stolen herd in some hidden ravine between the shouldering hills. Rowdy whistled softly. When a fellow was getting the legs run off him, it was some consolation, perhaps, to know who was making it hot for him, but Buckmaster's tenacity posed a new question. Why was the man so intent upon capturing them?

Not that Rowdy waited to contemplate this question in idleness. Not at all. He and his friends were sitting their saddles in the fringe of that first clump of timber along the wagon road, and Buckmaster had spied them, for guns began a raucous barking. The distance was far too great to make a six-shooter any real menace, but the continued popping of Colts counselled haste on Rowdy's part. He lifted his horse to a run, the others stringing out behind him again, and they headed southward, keeping to the road.

Buckmaster's bunch was still coming, and again the question arose in Rowdy's mind. Buckmaster's idea might be to cement his claim of innocence as concerned his own recent relationship with Butch Rafferty by turning this same Butch Rafferty triumphantly over to the law. Yet Butch

Rafferty, lodged in the Latigo calaboose along with his daughter, would be able to swear that he had indeed been forcibly taken from the Empire Hotel by Thane Buckmaster and held as an unwilling guest in the Eagle's Eyrie. Rowdy Dow would be able to substantiate that statement in part, and so would Clee Drummond. All of which would add up to acute embarrassment for Thane Buckmaster. Therefore it followed that Buckmaster was the one presumably law-abiding citizen of Latigo Basin who should be happy over Butch Rafferty's continued freedom—and silence. Yet Buckmaster persisted in raising this hue and cry.

More than that, the pursuers, having sighted their quarry, were desperately intent upon closing the distance, and they were belabouring their horses with telling results. Rowdy, mindful that continuing along this wagon road would bring him straight into Latigo town, veered now to the southeast, heading back toward the basin's towering wall, and Stumpy and the Raffertys spread out and rode abreast of him. The guns were kicking up dust dangerously close. Rowdy, casting a backward glance, saw that Buckmaster was gaining, but that alone was not all that Rowdy discovered that made a new strategy imperative.

"Get into the timber again!" he called to his companions as he worked hard at getting a fresh burst of speed from his horse.

Another backward glance showed him that the distance was beginning to widen between themselves and Buckmaster's bunch. Rowdy and his friends had rested their horses in the clump of trees, and Buckmaster had had no opportunity to do likewise. The pursuit had been able to hold its own and even to gain, but the miles were now telling on the Buckmaster mounts though the outfit clung to the trail with a tenacity that would have shamed a woodtick. Rowdy pushed forward, intent upon getting into screening timber, but when the trees were around them, he hauled hard on his reins and then piled from his saddle and ran toward Butch Rafferty who, like the others, upon seeing Rowdy stop had done likewise.

"Pile aboard my horse!" Rowdy ordered the veteran owlhooter. "And strip off that jumper you're wearing and give it to me. Hurry now!" Rafferty obviously didn't understand, but he obeyed. Rowdy swung aboard the piebald and said, "We'll split up here. You Raffertys head deeper into the timber and then lie low. Stumpy, you and me will show ourselves again."

Rafferty said, "But you're taking the piebald. They can spot that cayuse a mile off. You want them to think that you're me!"

"Right as rain," Rowdy admitted. "It's *you* they're after. Didn't you notice the shooting when we were riding abreast? One of us made as good a target as another, but every cap that was cracked was aimed at you. Buckmaster was playing it smart when he gave you the piebald. He was making sure you'd be forking a horse he could recognise easily if he got a glimpse of it later. Buckmaster isn't trying to capture you. For some reason he wants you dead."

Myra, still aboard her own heaving horse, said, "And you're going back out into the basin to deliberately draw their bullets——?"

"I'm not getting my hide punctured if I can help it," Rowdy protested. "My idea is to keep within sight but out of bullet range so they'll think they're chasing Butch. Later, when I've given you folks time to get deep into the timber, I'll let Buckmaster know he's trailing the wrong man. There's no time for arguing! Get going! You remember that schoolhouse we passed coming down the mountain trail? Head for there when it seems safe. Me and Stumpy will join you as soon as the sign's right."

Myra reined her mount close to the piebald, and she said, "You're right. There's no time for arguing. You're likely doing the wisest thing." She lifted her arms and placed them around his neck, and her lips brushed Rowdy's unshaven cheek. "*Vaya con Dios,*" she said. "Go with God."

Rowdy was too startled for a moment to find a ready tongue. Then: "*Yippee!*" he shouted and, slipping on Rafferty's jumper, he sent the piebald plunging off through the trees and back toward the basin's open floor, Stumpy Grampis close behind him.

They didn't show themselves at once. They kept just within the timber, veering steadily southward, and then they swung out of the leafy concealment. At first Rowdy could catch no glimpse of the pursuit, and his throat tightened, for his fear was that Buckmaster's bunch was deep in the timber and on the trail of the Raffertys. Then he made out a dust cloud to the north, and he and Stumpy deliberately rested their horses until they could recognise mounts and riders. The guns began barking again.

And now the race was on once more. Rowdy kept low in his saddle, remembering that he was a taller man than Butch Rafferty and that Buckmaster must not recognise the deception. Rowdy was heading due west now, and Buckmaster's bunch spread out in a thin semi-circle again, and Rowdy saw their new intent. Unable to close the distance between themselves and their quarry, they were going to herd the fugitives toward Latigo town. But soon Rowdy and his partner were into a tangled terrain of buttes and coulees, that same broken country that had made the lights of Latigo so elusive the night Stumpy and Bat Stull had ridden this way, presumably to get the china stallion from Latigo's post office. Often Buckmaster's bunch was lost from view, but always they appeared again, and soon Rowdy realised that he'd lost track of both time and distance and that he was nearly to the outskirts of town.

Rounding a bluff, he found the fair grounds ahead of him, a sea of tents with the globular bulk of the ascension balloon looming above everything else. Rowdy, reining to an abrupt halt, wondered then if he dared skirt the town, risking a chance that he wouldn't be recognised and find fresh pursuit on the trail. Then, suddenly, Buckmaster's bunch came streaming around the bluff, and there was no choice but to keep moving. The distance between pursuers and pursued had narrowed to almost nothing, and a throaty roar went up from Buckmaster's bunch, and Rowdy's name was in that roar. They knew now that they'd been deceived, those men, but still the guns spoke, and Stumpy's horse reared frantically and went down.

Instantly Rowdy was hauling his partner up behind him, and at the same time Rowdy fed the spurs to his mount. The burdened horse went lurching toward the fair grounds, and Rowdy knew then that this race was as good as lost. For in a knot of men who stood off at an angle from Rowdy's course was Sheriff Slim Pickens, recognisable in spite of a long wig and a putty nose he was wearing to-day, and that worthy had already sighted the oncoming pair.

This, Rowdy conceded, was one fine fix. He came out of the saddle, Stumpy alighting with him, and at the same time

Stumpy stumbled and went down. Rowdy hauled his partner erect and they went running, oblivious to the drumming of hoofs behind them, the peppering bullets and the wild shout of recognition from Slim Pickens. Dodging among tents and booths, Rowdy frantically sought durable cover, but now it seemed that men were everywhere, hurrying to intercept them, dodging in and out among the litter of tents, hopping over supporting ropes.

And then Rowdy found the way barred by a long iron flue mounted upon brick supports. Under the flue roared a great fire, but that fire had served its purpose, for the ascension balloon had been inflated by the heated air from the flue and had even risen a few feet above the ground. But the balloon was held down by many supporting ropes, their ends in the eager hands of a crowd of onlookers, mostly boys, who had volunteered for this chore. From the net of cordage that enclosed the inflated bag, a stout rope reached to the biggest windlass Rowdy had ever seen, the rope making several turns around the windlass and then trailing off into a coil that was obviously long enough to provide hobbles for all the horses in Montana.

This was a captive balloon, lifted by hot air and held anchored above the earth, when it ascended, by the rope and the windlass. Thus it was not to be the prey of every vagrant breeze once it was aloft. None of which meant anything to Rowdy Dow, whose knowledge of balloons was so infinitesimal as to be practically nonexistent. But he could recognise sanctuary in an hour of stress—and this, for want of better, was it. Pushing through the spectators, he grasped at the wicker basket suspended below the balloon and steadied it. "Climb in, Stumpy!" he urged hoarsely.

Stumpy looked dubious, and Rowdy said, "Climb in, man! Those boys of Buckmaster's were shooting for keeps! This will beat a bullet in the back!"

Before anyone could move to stop them, Stumpy had clambered aboard, and Rowdy piled in after him. The balloonist, a man in spangled tights, came running, spluttering explosively in what Rowdy judged to be French, but Rowdy had his gun in his hand now, and he swung it in a great arc. "Let go of those ropes!" he ordered. "Let go, I say. All of you!"

The balloonist had fallen back a pace, his waxed

moustache twitching in terror. It had taken a handsome bonus to entice him to fetch his act this far west, and he had alternately worried about his purse and his scalp ever since crossing the Mississippi. And every fear that had tortured him at the prospect of putting on a show back of beyond was symbolised by that gun in Rowdy's hand. Here, obviously, was a road agent in the flesh. And the boys and men who held the ropes were equally dominated, though in a different way. They knew you didn't argue with a man with a gun. The ropes, released, came slithering to the ground, and the balloon began rising. The brake wasn't on the windlass, and Rowdy saw the handle spin wildly. And also he saw the startled face of Thane Buckmaster as the man came pushing through the crowd, Bat Stull at his heels.

Buckmaster had grasped the situation. And Buckmaster, flourishing his own gun, was bellowing wild orders, his commands sending men racing to the windlass. Rowdy knew then what was up, and he saw the one flaw in his proposed plan to escape the fair grounds. Stout hands on that windlass would mean that the balloon would be held to the earth.

There was no time now to calculate the results of the only act that would be their saving. There was only time to do what had to be done. Leaning from the basket, Rowdy grasped at the anchoring rope that ran down to the windlass, held the rope taut and pressed his gun barrel against it and fired. The rope parted, and the balloon shot upward with startling suddenness. And Rowdy, who'd conceived a plan and put it through so quickly, wondered then, too late, if he'd been wise in choosing such an escape rather than the consequences of capture.

15. Brothers of the Birds

IT HAS BEEN said that any man who has built a fire and watched the smoke and hot air rise can understand the principles of a hot air balloon. In this respect, at least, both Rowdy Dow and Stumpy Grampis qualified as aeronauts. They'd built many a fire. But no one had ever explained to them that fire expands air, making it less dense than cold air, and the hot air, being lighter, rises accordingly. Nor had their education included the fact that hot air, enclosed in a balloon, lifts the balloon, once whatever binds it to the earth is released. Rowdy had realised that the rope and windlass held the balloon captive. He had severed the rope, and that action had converted their present conveyance into a free balloon, which, when aloft, is prey to the caprice of every passing wind. A free balloon, it may be conceded, is not a very practical vehicle for a person with a definite destination in mind.

More important, although Rowdy was familiar with the ancient adage that what goes up must inevitably come down, he had no conception as to how the balloon was to be brought back to earth. That was why, the instant he'd severed the anchoring rope, he regretted his action. But he had little opportunity to rue the day. Below him he glimpsed milling men, their faces turned upward and their mouths agape, and Rowdy found it odd that his sensation was not that he was ascending but that he was anchored in mid-air and the earth was falling away. Then he could see both the fair grounds and the town itself, and he even caught the glint of afternoon sunlight on the brass cannon on the courthouse lawn. The basin quickly spread below him, looking for all the world like a coloured map; he could make out roads and creeks and see the blotches that were clumps of trees. But the ground was falling away altogether too swiftly, and Rowdy's head began ringing, and suddenly he settled down to the bottom of the wicker basket and into unconsciousness. His last thought was that it was odd that Stumpy Grampis was underneath him and sleeping at a time like this.

Fortunately a free balloon does not continue to rise indefinitely. Learned men have it that it ascends to the level at which the rarefied air it displaces is just equal to the weight of the balloon, and here it stays until the air within the bag, cooling, grows heavier, whereupon it slowly settles earthward. But once a balloon has risen fifteen thousand feet above sea-level, its occupants are either going to be feeling the need for red flannel underwear or a breath of fresh air. Whether the height of the ascent or the quickness of it were responsible for the lapsing of Rowdy and his partner into unconsciousness, neither of them were ever to know. They recovered at practically the same time, their hearts pounding and their breath coming hard, and for a while they were content to lie entwined in the bottom of the basket, staring up at the great underbelly of the balloon and the dangling appendix into which the hot air had been forced.

Stumpy said then, "Dang it all, Rowdy, I told you once that I'm getting too old for the sort of fool nonsense a feller runs into when he's taggin' around with you!"

Rowdy attempted to pull himself erect and found this to be a sizeable feat under the circumstances, but he made it. Taking a steadying hold on one of the suspension lines that kept the basket slung beneath the balloon, he helped Stumpy get hoisted to a stand. Below spread the basin—far, far below, and Rowdy judged that they'd been drifting due west from Latigo town, and he wondered then, with some concern, what it would be like to come up against the peaks that made a spiked rampart a scant few miles away. Stumpy had a look too, sucked in his breath and said, "Son, this is nearer to heaven than I ever reckoned I'd get. First time I ever looked *down* on a hawk that was flying. You figger a fellow could cover the distance to the ground in *one* jump?"

"You stay here in the basket," Rowdy said firmly.

Yet all the while he was wrestling with the same problem, to which Stumpy had seen only one simple solution. Obviously getting down from a balloon required a different type of skill than piling off a cayuse. That the contraption was provided with a valve at its top which could be controlled from the basket, thus allowing air to escape at the aeronaut's will, Rowdy didn't know, and even if he had, he'd have hesitated to experiment with it. Ballast bags hung suspended from the sides of the basket, and Rowdy did free one of these and let it go plummeting earthward, but, to his consternation, this made the balloon rise instead of descend.

After that they both resigned themselves to circumstance. The balloon continued drifting, ever westward, and Rowdy, scanning the country below, made out the darker blotches of brown that were grazing cattle. Then he took to fixing his eyes on a certain peak in that wall to the west, and after due time he became convinced that the balloon was settling, if ever so slowly. Either that, or the mountain had started growing.

He began looking for horsemen, for he supposed that Thane Buckmaster, along with Bat Stull and the others, had probably taken to saddles and would be following along with the idea of being on hand when the balloon landed. Slim Pickens would likely be of the same mind, and Rowdy wondered if any posse in the past had ever pursued a free balloon. If history were being made, the newspapers might soon be mentioning Rowdy Dow again, and he wished he'd had a better picture taken of himself. But there were no horsemen to be seen, and Rowdy decided that perhaps the balloon had been drifting a great deal faster than it seemed, thus discouraging pursuit.

Rowdy was now beginning to enjoy himself. Convinced that the balloon was eventually going to settle to earth, his only concern was that it mustn't settle too abruptly and that he didn't want to land in a treetop when it did. Also, he was faced with the prospect that he and his partner were in for a bit of walking when they landed, and he remembered the schoolhouse and his rendezvous with the Raffertys. He tried to glimpse the schoolhouse, but it was on the far eastern side of the basin, and the balloon wasn't much over five hundred feet in the air now, and the visibility was limited. And suddenly Stumpy was tugging at his elbow and shouting hoarsely and pointing earthward.

Below them was a narrow ravine, pinched almost shut at either end and made by the crowding of two hills against each other. The eastern and nearer entry of the ravine angled inward in such a manner that horsemen riding the basin's floor might pass this way and never see it. But from above the view was perfection itself. Inside the ravine hundreds of cattle milled, held in check by only two riders whose labours had been limited to guarding either end of the ravine. Those riders had spied the balloon, for both were gaping upward, and Rowdy, leaning precariously over the basket's edge, shouted a greeting. But the cattle had sighted the balloon too, and there was imminent danger of a stampede, and the riders were suddenly concerned with holding the beef.

"Take a real look, Rowdy!" Stumpy was shouting, still plucking at his partner's sleeve. "I can't be certain about the men, but I shore recognise them horses they're forking. Those are two of Bat Stull's boys—the pair that wasn't with Stull and Buckmaster when they was runnin' the legs off us this morning."

Whereupon Rowdy realised the whole truth, and he said, "And those critters are the herd the basin ranchers lost the other night! Stumpy, we've found it!"

That was it. They'd come upon the secret of the vanished herd; they had cut sign where there'd been no sign, for that herd had been rustled during a rainstorm that had effectively washed away all evidence of its passage. Stull's men, acting under Buckmaster's orders, had rustled those cattle and moved them to this hidden ravine and were holding them here. Thus had Buckmaster hoped to blast the chances of the basin ranchers, keeping them from raising the money they needed to repay him if they were to retain their ranches—ranches which had suddenly become of great value with the advent of the railroad into the basin. Probably Buckmaster himself, or Curly Bill Callaghan, had known of this remote ravine and instructed Stull and his men to fetch the cattle here. But the secret was no longer a secret.

Rowdy and his partner had done what frantic basin riders had failed to do, and the basin men obviously hadn't even been making a search in the right locality, for Rowdy had seen no horsemen in this end of the basin. Rowdy wondered then why Sheriff Pickens or others hadn't thought of the efficiency of searching for the stolen cattle by balloon. Rustlers didn't stand the chance of a snowball in a depot stove when they were scouted by air. Then it occurred to

Rowdy that he himself hadn't seen the possibilities of the balloon. His ascension had had nothing to do with stolen cattle.

But they'd found those cattle, just the same. And Rowdy, in high glee, released another ballast bag and let it go plummeting downward. It landed just within the entrance of the ravine, spurting up dust and putting new fear into the cattle. But the balloon lifted again, lifted to a different strata of air, and then, perversely, it began drifting to the northeast. The ravine slipped from view, and Rowdy had a hard time picking it out again. The balloon seemed to be moving faster than ever, but Rowdy was concentrating on memorising the landscape, firmly fixing the outline of the hills in his mind, noting the position of tree clumps which might identify this location later.

The afternoon was far gone now, and Rowdy became mindful that it had been a long time between meals. He wondered if the coming of darkness made any difference to a balloon, but, in any case, the huge bag was settling almost as fast as the sun. Now Rowdy could clearly see the wagon road, far off to the east, and he saw a spread of buildings below and made out men darting frantically across the ground and pointing upward, and he saw those same men mounting horses. This was Crenshaw's ranch, but it was a few minutes before Rowdy realised it; the place looked entirely unfamiliar from above. By the time he was certain, the balloon had drifted on to the northeast.

There was one consolation in this: when it finally settled down, it wasn't going to land on a mountain top. True, there were those intermittent clumps of trees below, but, with a little luck, they'd avoid them. And each passing minute was making the two amateur aeronauts more acutely aware that the time they would remain aloft was limited.

Then, almost abruptly it seemed, the wicker basket was scraping the ground and tilting over, and Rowdy and his partner found themselves smothered beneath the collapsing bag. Tangled in the lines and netting, they fought frantically to extricate themselves, and they came out clawing from beneath all this impedimenta to find themselves upon the naked prairie.

"The next time," said Stumpy with an explosive sigh,

"that I gotta choose between a bullet in the brisket or a ride in a balloon, I'm takin' the bullet."

"We might as well start walking," Rowdy decided, and pointed due east. "I make it out that the schoolhouse is yonder in that direction."

But they hadn't put over a quarter of a mile between themselves and the balloon when they saw dust boiling to the southeast, a reddish-gold cloud in the last rays of the sun, and they stopped then, resignedly, knowing that they couldn't outrun mounted horsemen. When those riders came roaring to a stop, surrounding them, John Crenshaw, a big man upon a big horse, eyed the pair in open amazement. "We saw the balloon," Crenshaw said. "We figured that the Frenchman had got cut loose from his tether, though some of the boys swore there were two fellows in the basket. What in thunderation were you and Grampis doing up there?"

Clee Drummond was in the group, looking much like his former self except that the white of a bandage showed beneath his sombrero. He fixed his sleepy-eyed gaze upon the pair and said, "Howdy, boys. You're a problem. What are we going to do with you now that we've come across you? You've been hiding out with Butch Rafferty; Stumpy admitted that to us last night. Even if I've shed my badge, I can't go on overlooking that. The first thing you know, Slim Pickens will have *me* locked up for siding the pair of you."

Rowdy grinned. "You're going to let us go, Drummond, and no questions asked," he said. "You're even going to lend us a couple of those cayuses. You can tell Pickens we got 'em at gun-point, if any questions are asked. In fact you're going to be mighty nice and polite to us, old hoss. Because we're the boys who can tell you the whereabouts of that beef herd that walked away on you the other night."

Crenshaw was the quickest to recognise the truth. "You spotted it from the balloon!"

"Right as rain," said Rowdy. "Look." Kneeling, he began tracing a map in the ground with his index finger, and as he worked he talked. When he'd finished, Crenshaw said, "I know where you mean. So the rustlers took the stock south! We'd all guessed that they'd moved north; the far end of the basin is pretty wild country. And you say there's only two men holding them? They saw the balloon, of course. But they won't have had time to move the cattle far, and the chances are they haven't dared—not in daylight. Boys, we'll have that herd in Latigo before the night's over.''

Rowdy said, ''If you can spare some men and a wagon. I'll appreciate it if you'll tote that balloon back to town. I'd hate to have to pay for it. Now how about those saddlers for us?''

Crenshaw was so highly elated that Rowdy could have had a platinum saddle for the asking, if one had been available, and, at a nod from the banker-rancher, two of his men stepped down from their horses and hoisted themselves up behind other riders. When Rowdy and his partner were mounted, Drummond said, ''The bargain was that there were to be no questions asked, Rowdy. But if you should just *happen* to see Butch Rafferty, you'd be doing him a favour if you talked him into surrendering himself. I still think I can get the governor to consider a pardon. But every day that Butch's loose from stony lonesome will make it that much harder.''

Rowdy winked. ''If I run across him, I'll give him your love.''

Then he and Stumpy were lifting their mounts and heading eastward, while Crenshaw's men veered off toward the southeast, their destination obviously that hidden ravine where the stolen herd was held, and their haste indicative of their desire to cover the miles in a mighty hurry. The dusk came swooping down, and there was a mutter of thunder in the northern hills, where the basin's walls pinched together. Rowdy and Stumpy rode at a hard gallop toward the school-house.

''Whatever happened to the Raffertys,'' Rowdy said, ''I hope they hung onto that grub-sack that was tied to my saddlehorn when we switched horses.''

Deep dark was upon the land when they came within sight of the schoolhouse. There were no horses at the hitchrack, but Rowdy hadn't expected any; Rafferty was far too wily to leave such obvious evidence of his presence. Nor was there any light showing in the windows of the structure, but as Rowdy cautiously circled the building, he thought he detected a faint glimmer at one window on the far side.

Coming down from his saddle and motioning to Stumpy to do likewise, the two crept carefully forward.

"Someone's inside, and I'm betting that it's the Raffertys," Rowdy whispered. "They've drawn the shades and hung a saddle blanket over the window nearest the lamp. Let's have a peek."

But when Rowdy doffed his sombrero and placed his eye to the window, he had one look and stepped back with a low-voiced ejaculation. "There's people inside," he whispered. "Two or three. I could hear them moving around. But there's only one I could see from where I stood."

"Butch Rafferty?"

"No," said Rowdy. "Stonehead Jackson. Something's mighty wrong."

16. Stonehead Speaks

STONEHEAD JACKSON HAD BEEN with Bat Stull and the others who had ridden at Thane Buckmaster's back in relentless pursuit of Rowdy and his friends earlier to-day. Rowdy had recognised the bigness of the giant on more than one occasion. And now Jackson was here, in the basin schoolhouse. Rowdy's obvious conclusion, then, was that Bat Stull's men had turned back from Latigo after Rowdy and his partner had escaped by means of the balloon, returned again to the schoolhouse where once they'd quartered, and that all of them were inside at this very moment. But what of Butch Rafferty and Myra? That was Rowdy's real concern. The Raffertys were to have met him here, and the question was whether the outlaw and his daughter were also inside, prisoners of Bat Stull's bunch.

There was only one way to learn the truth, and Rowdy instantly began cat-footing around the building toward the doorway, Stumpy silently padding behind him. En route, they tried peering into other windows, but the shades were too tightly drawn. At the door, Rowdy freed his gun, and with the six-shooter in his right hand, he put his left to the knob, turned it silently and then lunged into the building. It proved to be a most anti-climactic moment.

Three people were inside, and one of them was Stonehead Jackson. No mistake about that. The giant was seated on a desk, and he had a beer bottle in his hand—that same beer bottle Rowdy had found in the cloak room. Jackson was holding the bottle up to his eye and squinting down the neck suspiciously, and Butch Rafferty and Myra were silently watching him. There wasn't another soul in sight.

Rafferty reacted the swiftest to Rowdy's startling entry.

The veteran owlhooter spun, falling into a crouch at the same time, and his right hand dropped to his thigh. He wore no gun, and he seemed to realise this fact at the same moment that he recognised Rowdy, for he grinned sheepishly. Panic had come into Myra's eyes, but it was quickly replaced by a show of elation that was very gratifying to Rowdy. Only Jackson regarded the newcomers with stoical indifference. If he bore any animosity toward Rowdy from their last direct meeting, the occasion when Rowdy had borrowed Jackson's gun and laid the barrel across the giant's skull, Jackson didn't show it. Jackson had another gun now, but he made no move toward it.

Butch Rafferty said, "Dow! So you and Stumpy got through safe! Stonehead's been babbling some wild story about the two of you escaping Buckmaster by taking off in an ascension balloon. I'm mighty glad to see you."

None of this was as Rowdy had expected it to be, and suspicion and fear were still strong in him. "Where's the rest of Stull's outfit?" he demanded.

"In Latigo, I'd guess," Rafferty said. "Stonehead walked in here no more than half an hour ago. He says he left the others in town."

"You mean that Jackson has quit Stull's bunch?"

Rafferty nodded. "So he says. Take it easy, Dow. There's no need to worry about this big fellow. I knew him well in Deer Lodge pen. In fact, he had the bed next to mine in the prison hospital."

"I'd forgotten," Rowdy said. "Do you mean that Jackson's lined up with you against Stull?"

Rafferty shook his head. "Jackson just happened to stumble onto us here. The big fellow is heading out of the country. Stull's got in deep, and Jackson's afraid that if he sticks with Stull, he'll end up back in the pen. Jackson had enough of stony lonesome while he was there. And he's told us all about Stull's deal with Buckmaster."

"Me, I'd like to hear about that," Rowdy said.

Stumpy, a silent listener up until now, said, "Me, I'd like something to eat. And pronto. Did you folks fetch that grubsack?"

The sack was in a corner, and Myra Rafferty went to it at once and began preparing food. Rowdy cased his gun and perched himself atop a desk. "Jackson told it straight about the balloon," he said. "It's a long story, and I wouldn't expect you to believe it anyway. Now that it's over, I don't even believe it myself. What Jackson has had to say is likely more interesting. I'm listening, Butch."

Jackson had put the beer bottle aside in obvious disappointment and had drawn the copy of the *Arabian Nights* from his shirt front. He was deep in the book and paying absolutely no heed to the others as Butch Rafferty shot a glance toward the giant. "Jackson's a simple sort of galoot," Rafferty said. "But he's got one mighty queer gift. It used to startle us in prison. He can recite any talk he's ever heard. Most of what I've gotten from him to-night has been the talk of other men. But from it, I've pieced out just about everything that's happened."

Rowdy nodded. "I've seen him perform."

"Seems that Bat Stull discovered that Sam Usher had disappeared from the basin," Rafferty went on. "That meant that Stull's hope of getting the loot I'd left with Usher was blasted. So Stull decided to call the game quits and get out of the basin. But on his way up over Latigo Pass, he stopped at Thane Buckmaster's to beg a meal."

Myra brought food to Rowdy and his partner, and Rowdy thanked her with his eyes. "And Buckmaster recognised the snake streak in friend Bat and offered him a job," Rowdy suggested.

"That was about the size of it," Rafferty agreed. "But the work was likely to take Stull further beyond the law than he'd ever had the guts to go. So Buckmaster had to convert him. Buckmaster has been in the money-lending business here in competition to John Crenshaw, so naturally Buckmaster hasn't been using Crenshaw's bank. In fact, Buckmaster keeps his money underneath the Eagle's Eyrie, in a regular vault. Buckmaster and Callaghan talked Stull's boys into putting their guns aside, and then, when they'd got them de-fanged so that Stull wasn't likely to try a holdup, Buckmaster took them down into the cellar and showed them money—stacks of currency. I gather that Stull's eyes just about popped out and rolled across the floor. But it was the right kind of medicine. One long look at all that dinero, so near and yet so far, and Stull decided that Thane Buckmaster was the gent to string along with."

Rowdy essayed speech, but his mouth was too full for a

moment. "My next guess is that Buckmaster had the first job for Stull's boys already in mind," Rowdy managed to say. "Buckmaster had likely gotten wind that the Latigo ranchers were gathering beef to sell to the railroad. It was no secret anyway. And we know why Buckmaster didn't want money in the ranchers' pockets."

"That's it, Rowdy. And it was Stull's bunch who run off the herd the other night. Jackson admitted that—he even had a hand in it. That's what got the big galoot worried. Stull left a couple of his boys to watch the herd, and the rest came back to the Eagle's Eyrie. They were there when Stumpy came back up the trail from Crenshaw's early this morning with yonder grub-sack. Stumpy was spotted, and they followed him, figgering he'd lead them to the rest of us."

"And *you* in particular. Did Jackson say why Buckmaster is so all fired anxious to tack your hide to the wall?"

Rafferty shook his head. "Jackson doesn't know. But Jackson was with those boys when they chased us down out of the hills this morning. That was just about the last straw for the big fellow. He's thick in the head, but not so thick but what he can figger out that Stull is getting in deeper and deeper all along. That's why Jackson is running out."

Rowdy said, "There's no need for that. Jackson has shown how he really stands by wanting to shake loose from Stull. Once all this trouble is settled, I think I can get him a job at John Crenshaw's ranch. And the trouble will be settled mighty soon. Me and Stumpy spotted that missing herd, Butch. John Crenshaw and his crew are on their way after it right now. They'll likely have it in Latigo to-night. I reckon that Thane Buckmaster has played his last hand."

"What do *we* do next?" Rafferty asked.

Rowdy sighed. "Me, I've had a busy day. Right now I can't think of anything better than stretching out and getting some sleep. There's thunder over the hills, and it looks like rain, and I'm in favour of keeping this roof over us. The only thing we've got to worry about is Bat Stull's bunch. But likely they won't drop in here. Either they'll stay in town or head back to the Eagle's Eyrie."

Stumpy made a departure and returned in due time bearing saddle blankets. "Hid Crenshaw's hosses out in the deep timber," he told Rowdy. "Once we get the lamp out, there'll be no sign that anybody's here, no matter how close

Stull might look if he happens to go riding up the mountain to-night. Let's grab some shut-eye.''

And so it was decided, for they were all of the same mind, and they'd had a strenuous time between suns. Even Stonehead Jackson, yawning widely, was content to put Scheherazade's tales aside and stretch upon the floor. Rowdy slept with his gun at his fingertips and half of his consciousness standing sentinel against any alien noise in the night.

The rain never came, though sometimes the thunder muttered, and Rowdy woke intermittently, vaguely ill at ease. He tried to analyse this feeling; he had learned to give heed to such nameless instincts, but there was no logic that he could locate. It had been a good day, he remembered, for hadn't they found the stolen herd? Yet Thane Buckmaster was in his mind, and he recalled his first impression of the man, formed aboard the train out of Jubilee. He'd sensed a driving power in Buckmaster, and he knew now that his fear was that Thane Buckmaster was not yet beaten.

Butch Rafferty, the last to bed down, had raised the shades once the lamp was extinguished, and the dawn light, greying the windows, woke Rowdy at an early hour. For a time he was content to lie upon the blanket, his head pillowed upon his sombrero, listening to the even breathing of Myra who slept nearby, the calliope-like snoring of Stumpy Grampis. Then he became aware that someone was talking, and he rolled on his side to have a look at Stonehead Jackson.

The giant lay upon the floor, his hands hooked at the back of his head, and Jackson was staring at the ceiling and was off on one of those aimless recitals of his. And, listening, Rowdy's interest quickened. '' 'I've drawn a map for you, Stull,' '' Jackson said in that flat and lifeless voice of his. '' 'It shows you the basin, and you'll find any number of coulees down in the southwestern end that will serve your purpose. Run the herd into one of them, and leave a couple of men to hold it.' ''

That, Rowdy realised, had been Thane Buckmaster talking.

'' 'Don't be afraid of running the tallow off those cattle,' '' Jackson went on. '' 'It isn't as though we were stealing the herd in order to sell it. The main idea is merely to hide it away so the basin ranchers won't be able to deliver. Is that idea clear to all you men? If anybody shows up while you're holding the herd, don't make a fight. Take to your heels instead, and keep from being recognised if you can. You have the advantage of being strangers here. Dow and his friends know you're working for me, but they're hiding out in the hills. We'll have no trouble from them.' "

Rowdy was all ears. No wonder Buckmaster hadn't been happy over Rowdy's discovery that Stull's bunch was working for the man that day Rowdy had taken Butch Rafferty from the Eyrie. Now Stumpy Grampis's snoring had suddenly ceased, and Rowdy knew without looking that Stumpy had come awake and was listening. And, somewhere beyond Rowdy's range of vision, Butch Rafferty drew in a long breath. To Rowdy this was a skin-prickling experience. He had known of Jackson's weird talent, and he'd heard the man recite before. But those had been fragmentary, aimless things. This was as though the giant had borrowed another man's intelligence; he had Stonehead Jackson's body and voice, but the brain had become Thane Buckmaster's.

" 'I'm counting on that herd staying lost until it's too late for its recovery to mean anything,' " Jackson droned. " 'If there's a slip, we've still one ace to play. The ranchers may recover the cattle and collect railroad money, but we'll see to it that they don't keep the money long enough to be able to do business with it. Now you'd better get riding, men. It will be after dark by the time you get down into the basin.' "

Rowdy was easing into his boots as Jackson finished his speech. Butch Rafferty, propped upon one elbow, said, "What do you make of it?"

"Plenty!" Rowdy said. "Myra, you awake? Can you build us a breakfast in a hurry? Stumpy, get those boots on. You and me are taking a ride."

He glanced again at Rafferty. "You and Myra stay here," Rowdy said. "You'll be as safe in this schoolhouse as any place, likely, and I don't think you'll be seeing Bat Stull hereabouts. Bat's going to be a busy little feller, unless I miss my guess. No wonder Jackson wanted to shake loose from him! Do you see Buckmaster's idea? He guessed that the herd might be discovered. So he planned in advance. I'm going to Latigo to find out what's happened since I last saw John Crenshaw."

"What about Jackson?" Rafferty asked.

"Keep him here. Maybe he'll do some more talking from time to time. I want somebody around listening if he does."

Myra was already delving into the grub-sack. "But you can't go into Latigo, Rowdy!" she protested. "You know the law's after you for helping Dad hide out."

"The law is the very party I'm going to see," Rowdy declared grimly. "It's time Slim Pickens got some sense pounded into his head. All I'm hoping is that I'm not too late. If Buckmaster has had Stull and his boys snatch that railroad money, the basin ranchers have lost their last chance to beat Buckmaster's game!"

17. The Muttering Mob

THE LAST TIME ROWDY DOW had ridden toward Latigo he'd had a gun-slinging pack at his heels, intent upon mayhem. With Stumpy Grampis at his side, Rowdy covered the miles just about as quickly this morning, a growing sense of urgency spurring him. Strong within Rowdy was the feeling that the real showdown was now shaping itself. Just exactly what he expected to find in Latigo, he couldn't have said. When the pair reached the outskirts of the town, Rowdy's only concessions to the need of making an unobtrusive entrance was the slowing of his horse to a walk and the tugging of his sombrero brim down over his eyes. These precautions taken, the two rode boldly into the main street.

It was late morning, an hour when Latigo should have been comparatively quiet. In an ordinary cowtown at this time there'd be a few bonneted shoppers upon the street, wending from mercantile to mercantile, a few children at play, a dozing dog or two. The saloons should have been deserted save for the swampers and the bartenders, for their business began building in the afternoon and rose to its peak in the evening. But these were not the prevailing conditions. A great many buckboards flanked the boardwalks, and the hitchrails were crowded with saddlers. Rowdy remembered the county fair, but he knew instantly that it wasn't the attraction of the midway or the exhibits that had drawn such a crowd. The saloons were reaping the harvest; every one of them was a-roar with activity.

Stumpy shivered. "Listen!" he said. "Hear that mutterin' sound underneath all the noise? The boys ain't liquorin' for fun. I've heard that mutter before, and a feller never forgets it. My guess is that somebody is in for a lynching."

Rowdy had detected that same ominous note, but he said nothing. His nerves had been on trigger edge since they'd entered the town, for he was well aware that Thane Buckmaster's sly tongue had put them beyond the law and made them marked men. Yet the teeming activity of Latigo was in a sense a protection. People were too intent upon their own affairs to pay any heed to a pair of strangers. But that rumbling undercurrent of trouble was not to Rowdy's liking.

He had come to palaver with Sheriff Slim Pickens, and he supposed he'd find the lath-like lawman in the courthouse. Accordingly, Rowdy racked his horse before the sumptuous structure and started across the lawn where the brass cannon stood. Turning to make sure Stumpy was following him, Rowdy faced John Crenshaw's bank for a moment, and he was surprised to see the shades drawn in its big, fronting windows, and the door closed. But there were two saddlers at the bank's hitchrail, and both bore Crenshaw's brand.

Latigo was a realm of riddles to-day, but Slim Pickens likely had the answers. Into the courthouse, the pair came along an echoing hallway on the first floor, scanning the legends on the many office doors. They passed places where they might have procured marriage licences, paid delinquent taxes, or registered the advent of progeny, if such had been their intentions, and then they found the law's sanctuary. The door was slightly ajar, and Slim Pickens was moving about beyond it. Casting a hasty glance the length of the hallway, Rowdy saw that he and his partner had it to themselves. Then Rowdy lunged into the sheriff's office, Stumpy at his heels, and Rowdy slammed the door shut and put his back to it.

"Don't try for a gun, Slim," Rowdy hastily advised. "We don't want to have to shoot you. The fact is, we're here to lend you a hand."

Slim Pickens had been engaged in an odd occupation. This office was furnished with a roll-top desk, spur-scarred and burned by many cigarettes, a swivel chair, a battered filing cabinet, and a small stove. Although the day was warm, the air almost sultry, Pickens had a fire roaring in the stove. Its isinglassed door was open, and Pickens had been busily thrusting papers into the flames. Now he turned, his long arms dropping to his sides, and he regarded the pair not with surprise or anger but almost mournfully.

"I'm not after you galoots," he said. "Not any more. All I had against you was hearsay evidence that you've been helping Butch Rafferty hide out. From now on, I'm Missouri's favourite adopted son. I don't believe *nothing* unless it's shoved under my nose!"

Rowdy bristled with questions, but this about-face attitude of Pickens was so startling that he had to probe it further before he could put his trust in the man. "Now you're talking," Rowdy said. "I had you pegged for a square-shooter when I first met you, Pickens. But when Thane Buckmaster and Bat Stull chased me into town yesterday, you were as anxious as anybody to lay hands on me. If you'd really been keeping your badge polished, you'd have jailed Bat Stull and his bunch."

Pickens sighed. "I've listened to Thane Buckmaster, and I've listened to Clee Drummond. It made my head spin. I re-read all the lessons in a correspondence course I've been taking. It made my head worse. What have I got against Stull? Drummond says Stull stopped him in a Jubilee livery stable and searched him to the skin. But Drummond admits that Stull didn't take anything from him, though Drummond was packing money at the time. Seems to me that was a minor offence. It might have been different if Drummond had been wearing his federal marshal's badge. Then Stull would have been interfering with an officer."

"Dang it all!" Stumpy interjected. "Stull's bunch come aboard the train, masked and with guns in their hands, and they took me and Rowdy off that train. That ain't consti-tooshinal!"

"Logan MacLean told me about that deal," Pickens admitted. "But where's the proof? Thane Buckmaster was aboard that train, too. Yesterday, after you boys galloped off with the Frenchman's balloon, I asked Buckmaster if his crew wasn't the bunch MacLean had told me about. Buckmaster says they ain't. And MacLean was out of town yesterday, gone back to railroad division headquarters on business. He got here last evening on a special, and I talked to him again. According to his description, the leader of those men who boarded the train sure stacked up like Bat Stull. MacLean says he can identify him, mask or no mask.

But now Stull has skipped out. Ain't been seen since yesterday.''

Rowdy said, "Stull doesn't matter, anyway. MacLean can put the Injun sign on him and his bunch when the time comes. What I want to know is whether Crenshaw fetched that stolen herd in last night.''

Pickens nodded. "About midnight. And a couple of his boys brought in the balloon in a wagon. The Frenchman loaded it aboard a freight car and lit out of here so fast he left a trail of smoke behind him. I don't think he likes it this far west. Crenshaw said his crew had found the herd in a ravine over in the west wall after you boys spotted it from the air. That's another reason I'm not rattlin' handcuffs at you to-day. Couple of rustlers was holding the herd, but they took to the timber when Crenshaw's outfit showed up. That beef's been delivered. It's being held by the railroad on the flats south of the depot.''

Some of the tension went out of Rowdy. "Then Crenshaw's collected the money?''

"Logan MacLean brought the dinero back from division headquarters just on the chance that the herd might be found. He counted it out to Crenshaw in the depot last night, and I was there to act as witness. Crenshaw repped for all the ranchers who put up that beef.''

"Then the money is in Crenshaw's bank!'' Rowdy said exultantly.

Pickens shook his head. "Crenshaw started to his bank with it last night. He made the mistake of going alone. Somewhere this side of the depot, he got a gun-barrel laid between his ears. When he came awake again, the money was gone. He never even seen who hit him.''

Rowdy sagged weakly against the door, sick with the certainty that he'd foreseen Thane Buckmaster's next move but had come to Latigo too late to forestall it. If only Stonehead Jackson had taken to talking last evening! Rowdy said, "Don't you see, Slim? Buckmaster had that money stolen. Either he did it himself, or he had Bat Stull do it—just as he had Stull's men steal the herd. It's his last play to keep the ranchers from getting their hands on enough cash to lift that option he's holding. Go up to the Eagle's Eyrie and you'll find Crenshaw's money.''

"One greenback looks like another,'' Pickens said, and,

taking papers from his desk, he thrust them into the stove. "How can I make a charge against Buckmaster? No, don't get me wrong. I'm not blind any more. I can see the skunk stripe down the man's back, but I can't prove anything. That's where he's got me licked—got us all licked. And I can't leave town, anyway. My most important job to-day is right here."

"Those mobs that are liquoring in the saloons!" Rowdy guessed. "What's up, Pickens?"

"Devil's work," said the sheriff. "A lot of ranchers came in for the fair. Buckmaster and Curly Bill Callaghan are in town and buying drinks for anybody that's thirsty. The ranchers have learned, of course, that Crenshaw collected their money for them and never got to the bank with it. It's riled them considerable, and Buckmaster's talk is making them wilder. You see, if they stopped to think for a minute, or to listen to John Crenshaw, they'd realise that Buckmaster is the man who stands to gain by that money disappearing last night. Buckmaster knows that, so he's turning them against Crenshaw in order to turn them away from himself. Already there's talk of storming Crenshaw's bank and taking what money is left in the vault. A little more red-eye down their gullets and they'll be threatenin' to burn the bank building."

Rowdy said, "I noticed that the bank was closed and the shades drawn. But there are saddlers out front."

"John Crenshaw and Clee Drummond are over there, keeping the place locked and preparing to defend it if the ranchers really get pawin' up enough sod to attack. And that's why I'm staying in town. There's no use trying to talk to a bunch of men who've got their brains scrambled by whisky and suspicion. But if a play is made against Crenshaw, I'll be here to back him."

He thrust more papers into the fire, and Stumpy, his curiosity overpowering him, said, "What in thunder are you burning?"

"My correspondence course," Pickens said sadly. "I'm beginning to think that the more learnin' a feller has, the less he knows. I should have seen through Buckmaster months ago."

Rowdy, his lips gone grey, said, "So whisky is turning

the ranchers against Crenshaw—the best friend they've ever had. I can't believe it!''

"The trick wasn't turned in a single day," Pickens explained. "Buckmaster started a whispering campaign against Crenshaw years back. Kept pointing out that Crenshaw's bank was run on a shoestring and that it wasn't safe to keep money there. And it made a pretty good argument because folks knew that Crenshaw had never been sound since he'd had that money stolen by Butch Rafferty a long time ago. After last winter, when folks needed money, most of them didn't even bother to ask Crenshaw for loans. They went straight to Buckmaster and gave him that blanket option as security. Of course, when MacLean fetched a proposition direct to Crenshaw to get beef for the railroad, the ranchers obliged and gathered a herd when Crenshaw asked them to. But first the herd was stolen, and then the money disappeared. It don't make Crenshaw look very dependable, does it?''

Rowdy said, "Butch Rafferty was the most unselfish man I ever met. John Crenshaw ran him a close second. And this is the pay Crenshaw is to get from the very men he's been trying to save from being swindled!''

"Don't judge 'em too harshly," Pickens said. "They've had a hard year; they've seen hope dangled before 'em and then snatched away. All they know to-day is that their money is gone—the money they could have used to redeem their ranches. Buckmaster's poison has been slow, and that's made it all the more deadly. Crenshaw will forgive them for whatever they do before sundown. But Crenshaw will fight to defend his bank.''

Rowdy's eyes narrowed thoughtfully. "I came here to do a chore for Clee Drummond," he said. "You might say that chore was to deliver a china stallion, but the little horse was only a symbol of the real job. That job was to help out John Crenshaw—a thing that Butch Rafferty wanted done. The only thing that will make sense to those ranchers who are out yonder swilling Buckmaster's free liquor is money. But Sam Usher ran off with Crenshaw's money. By the way, Slim, did you ever get an answer to that telegram Crenshaw asked you to send to the Acme people asking them to check up on Usher at Ashland, Ohio?''

"Come this morning," Pickens said with no enthusiasm.

"Collect. Don't know whether the county will stand the cost."

He dug among the papers littering his desk and produced a thin yellow message. This he handed to Rowdy, who read:

INVESTIGATION REVEALS NO SAM USHER EVER LOCATED AT ASHLAND STOP YOUR DESCRIPTION OF THE MAN FITS ONE SAM BUCKNER WHO LEFT ASHLAND FIFTEEN YEARS AGO AFTER COMMITTING MURDER STOP SUGGEST YOU PUT SAM USHER IN CUSTODY AS THERE IS LIBERAL REWARD DEAD OR ALIVE AND HE MIGHT PROVE TO BE SAME MAN STOP HAVE YOU CONSIDERED TAKING OUR ADVANCED COURSE IN DETECTING AND CRIMINOLOGY STOP REDUCED RATES TO STUDENTS FINISHING PRELIMINARY TRAINING.

"Another dead end trail," Pickens sighed. "If Sam Usher murdered somebody in his home town before leaving it, naturally he never showed back there. I'm afraid John Crenshaw might as well figger that money's gone down a gopher hole."

Rowdy had absorbed the message, Stumpy reading over his shoulder, but Rowdy's thoughts had drifted elsewhere, and he'd grown grimmer. "We still need money to bring the ranchers to their senses," he said. "When Clee Drummond gave me this job, he told me he needed somebody with my talents. Maybe he spoke wiser than he knew. There's just one way I'd have handled this before the governor gave me a pardon. And that way will still work."

He turned to Stumpy. "Stay here with Pickens," Rowdy said. "He'll need all the help he can get if he has to side Crenshaw against a mob bent on tearing the bank apart. Me, I'll try to get back before deep dark."

"Where you going?" Stumpy asked.

Rowdy was already wrenching the door open. "To fight fire with fire," he said. "What you don't know, you'll never have to answer to on a witness stand. So long, pard."

18. The Stallion Again

THANE BUCKMASTER WAS NO longer in town, and neither was Curly Bill Callaghan. This Rowdy learned by making a quick round of the saloons. All of these fonts of refreshment were still packed with men, and Buckmaster, Rowdy discovered, had left money on the various bars to accommodate the thirst of the ranchers for many an hour. There was plenty of fuel still to be added to the fire, and the mood of the ranchers wasn't such as to indicate that any efforts to direct their feet to soberer paths would be met with enthusiasm. Each drinker had left a little of his wisdom in the bottom of an empty bottle, and that low and ominous mutter was growing increasingly louder.

There was, Rowdy recalled, an old saying that money talked. The question now was whether he could equip himself with the proper vocal chords in time to stave off the disaster that threatened John Crenshaw's bank. Yet Rowdy moved with slow and deliberate care. Having looked into the various saloons, he took a stand on the edge of a boardwalk and carefully scanned the street. Buckmaster's fancy surrey was not in sight, and therefore it was quite evident that Buckmaster had shaken the dust of Latigo from his fancy boots.

Whereupon Rowdy headed into a restaurant and had himself a man-sized meal. Thus reinforced, he went to the railroad depot and made certain inquiries. Yes, a pair of saddlers were on hand, shipped over the hump by the Jubilee livery stable. Leaving Stumpy's cayuse in the custody of the railroad, Rowdy mounted and headed out of Latigo along the road that led to the distant mountain pass.

It was the first time in many a day that Rowdy had had

his own private horse under him, and it gladdened him to
be aboard the mount again. They'd covered quite a few miles
together, these two, and Rowdy had had occasion to believe
that the horse could smell the tin of a sheriff's badge a mile
and a half away when the wind was right. Now Rowdy kept
the mount at a steady jog, his destination the Eagle's Eyrie.

He was like a man detached from himself, was Rowdy.
He knew exactly what he was going to do and how he was
going about it, and he was fully aware that he'd be forever
beyond the law when his mission was accomplished. Since
coming to Latigo Basin, he'd jeopardised the governor's
pardon by helping Butch Rafferty, and he'd done so
hesitantly, for the freedom represented by that piece of paper
meant something to him. Now nothing mattered but the need
to beat Thane Buckmaster.

The unselfishness of his present attitude, striking him,
brought a grin. The owlhoot had trained him to think first
of his own hide, and he wondered just how the change had
come about. Butch Rafferty was mixed into it, of course.
Rafferty and the ancient debt the Dows owed the man. And
Myra Rafferty was involved, too—Myra who had kissed him
just yesterday. And there was John Crenshaw who hadn't
wanted his neighbours swindled; and Clee Drummond who'd
laid aside a marshal's badge to help a friend. Even Slim
Pickens had turned out to be a good example, for Pickens,
bewildered by Buckmaster's sly tongue, was, at the
showdown, taking a man's stand.

Yes, this Latigo country certainly had a softening influence. Maybe it would be best to get out of the basin before
a fellow took to sitting in a rocker and knitting. Then Rowdy
remembered that he was going to have to leave this range—
and pronto—anyway. One last chore and the law would be
barking at his heels again. Maybe it was best that that picture
of his they used on reward dodgers wasn't such a good one
after all.

It began raining in mid-afternoon, before he reached the
schoolhouse; the storm that had threatened for the past
twenty-four hours had now made up its mind to get down
to business. There was a steady drizzle as Rowdy started up
the slant of the hill, and the thunder seemed to be moving
closer. He saw no signs of life about the schoolhouse when
he passed it, but he knew that Butch Rafferty and Myra were

inside, and likely Stonehead Jackson as well. Then he was beyond the building, and the wagon road snaked upward through the timber, and the rain no longer hit him as hard.

An early darkness, ushered in by the storm, was upon the land when Rowdy saw the lights of the Eagle's Eyrie glimmering through the trees. He had spared his horse on the trail; all his actions had been deliberate, for he was saving his mount and himself for a greater need that might yet come. But a growing urgency was in him as, dismounting, he led his horse into the timber flanking the trail. Drawing nearer to the cluster of buildings, he saw light shining from the cracks in the barn. Stull's outfit had been using the huge structure as a bunkhouse, so that meant that Stull's crew was here. Giving the barn reasonable berth, Rowdy ground-anchored his horse by that very clump of bushes which had once screened himself and his partner, and, as on that other occasion, he strode boldly toward the gallery fronting the house.

The front door was unlocked, and Rowdy eased into the hallway, a long, gloomy tunnel with light splashing into it from the open doorway leading to that high-ceilinged room where Rowdy twice before had found Thane Buckmaster. Talk hummed from beyond and then was lost in a peal of thunder that sounded so close it could have been up in the attic. That discordant crash would have blanketed his movements if Rowdy had fetched his horse into the house, so he came striding down the hall with no effort at silence.

He was into the room before he was discovered, but when he put his back to the wall, just inside the doorway, he had Stonehead Jackson's gun in his hand. Thane Buckmaster was seated in that great leather armchair, and Curly Bill Callaghan had his bulky legs thrust toward an open fireplace, and Bat Stull also filled a chair. A whisky decanter stood upon a low table, and the three had glasses in their hands. Buckmaster dropped his drink as he recognised the visitor.

"Don't bother getting up," Rowdy said. "And don't pour me a drink. This isn't a social call. I'm here to do business."

Buckmaster recovered himself enough to say, "Whatever you've got in your mind, Dow, you'll never get away with it. You're an outlaw now."

"You shouldn't have reminded me of that, mister,"

Rowdy said. "If I was dodging the law, it was because your snaky tongue put Pickens on my trail. But finish your drinks, boys. I'm happy you've got something in your right hands. It'll keep you from being tempted to try for a gun. Toasting your victory, Buckmaster? I left Latigo after you did, and the ranchers were still lapping up your free booze and making talk of tearing Crenshaw's bank apart. You've got something to celebrate, old son."

Curly Bill Callaghan was like a coiled spring, his prominent jaw had a petulant thrust to it, and he was leaning forward in his chair. But Rowdy was keeping a corner of his eye on Callaghan. Bat Stull lay limply in his chair, and fear dwelt in his small, piggish eyes. He was the least dangerous of the three. Thane Buckmaster would bear the most watching. Buckmaster had carefully picked up the glass he'd spilled, and now he filled it and hoisted it high. "You're right, Dow," he said. "I am celebrating. Just how much you know, I can only guess. It would seem to be enough. But nothing can be changed now. The fight is over, and the winner takes all."

"You spilled one glass before you got it to your lips," Rowdy observed. "Maybe that was an omen. But I'm taking up your time. I'll finish my business and be on my way. *I want that money you boys took from John Crenshaw last night!*"

Buckmaster lowered the untasted liquor. "You're talking nonsense!" he snapped.

"So? I can't prove you got that cattle money, is that it? But you know you got it—and I know, and that's enough for me. You see, Buckmaster, this isn't a court of law. We're doing business the owlhoot way. So trot out some folding money."

Buckmaster said, "A holdup, eh?"

"Look," said Rowdy, "I'm getting short of patience. Can't you savvy that I'm doing business *your* way. The only difference is that I'm being more direct. No sneaking and lying and poisoning right-minded people against a right-minded man. Short and to the point, that's me. Let's have that money!"

Buckmaster smiled. "Even if I had it, do you think I'd be such a fool as to keep large sums here in the house?"

"Where else?" Rowdy countered. "I've heard tell you've

got your own private bank vault underneath this buzzard's roost.''

That was like a body blow to Buckmaster; he winced visibly, his graven face loosing its imperturbability. Rowdy's voice became a whiplash. "Stand up! All of you! There, that's better.'' With the three on their feet, he moved cautiously forward, lifted Callaghan's gun from its holster and dropped it to the floor, did likewise with Bat Stull, and found a forty-five inside Buckmaster's coat.

"Now you boys form a line,'' Rowdy ordered. "That's right; you in the lead, Buckmaster. Bat, you and Callaghan place your hands on the shoulders of the man ahead of you. Buckmaster, lead the way, and I'll bring up the rear. We're having a look in the cellar. All set? January, February— *March!*''

Rowdy's gun prodding Buckmaster's ribs, the three lock-stepped toward the door, Callaghan nursing a murderous wrath, Stull displaying sullen fear, and Buckmaster gripped by a cold fury that was the most terrible of all. But now Rowdy found himself enjoying this to the hilt. The die was cast; he was an outlaw again by the law's standards, and there could be no turning back. All that was left was to make the most of the situation, and he was doing just that.

The four headed down the hallway, Rowdy keeping his gun ready and his eyes alert, and that left Buckmaster with no choice but to proceed to a door at the hall's end. His were the only hands that were free, and he opened this door and reached beyond it, a movement that instantly stiffened Rowdy. But Buckmaster was only reaching for a kerosene lamp which stood on a little shelf just inside the doorway. Rowdy supplied a match, and, when the lamp was aglow, said, "Here, I'll carry that. You might get nervous and throw it. At me.''

The light revealed steps leading downward. The passage was narrow, and Rowdy had to let the others precede him, but there was no chance for them to slip out of sight, for there was no turn in the stairs and, at the bottom, the group found itself in a little room, musty and dank and carved out of the solid rock upon which this house was founded. A ponderous iron door with a dial centring it was set in one wall—a door such as might have been found on any conventional bank vault. This, then, was the hidden treasure trove where Buckmaster had taken Bat Stull and his crew to impress them with his wealth and to enlist their aid in his scheming—the room Stonehead Jackson had told Butch Rafferty about.

Its only furnishings were a small, crude table and a keg with a gunny-sack folded upon it for padding, thus converting it into a seat. Rowdy placed the lamp upon the table, the shadows dancing weirdly upon the wall. "Callaghan, you and Stull get over there and put your bellies to the stone," Rowdy ordered. "That's right. Keep your hands high. O.K., Buckmaster. Let's see you spin that dial."

This was the telling moment, and in Buckmaster there was more fury than it was good for a man to possess. Doubtless he alone knew the combination of the vault, and if he refused to open the vault, Rowdy was going to lose precious time making him do so. The tension now was almost tangible, and out of it Bat Stull's voice quavered. "Don't open it, Buckmaster!" Stull cried. "He won't shoot. I know him, and I know his rep. He ain't got it in him to cut us down in cold blood!"

"No?" Rowdy barked. "Maybe not. But at this distance I could shoot an ear off each of you and still have three slugs left. Do you boys want to go through life lop-sided?"

Buckmaster stepped to the vault door. His fingers touched the dial and began manipulating it, and the only sound in this subterranean room was the clicking of the dial, the falling of tumblers. Buckmaster seemed an inordinately long time at the task, and Rowdy felt a rind of sweat grow upon his own upper lip. And then Buckmaster swung open the door. He was about to thrust a hand inside when Rowdy stopped him.

"Me first," said Rowdy. Reaching into the vault, he felt the crispness of packaged currency beneath his finger tips, but he also felt the hard outlines of a gun. Withdrawing the weapon, a loaded forty-five, he jacked the shells out of it and dumped the gun into a corner. "I expected something like this," Rowdy said. "You gave in too easy when I asked you to open the vault. Now, let's see—there were a thousand head of cattle delivered, and I reckon the market price these days is around forty bucks a head. That would be forty thousand dollars. I'll take it in twenties, fifties, and hundred dollar bills." He jerked the gunny sack from the top of the keg and extended the sack to Buckmaster. "You fill it. I'll count."

If ever there was murder in a man, it was in Buckmaster now; Rowdy could see it standing naked in Buckmaster's eyes. But still the gun was steady in Rowdy's hand, and still there was no choice, so Buckmaster began silently leafing through packages of currency and dumping them into the sack. Above the house the thunder spoke, distant and dim, and sometimes the lamp seemed to shiver, and the heavy breathing of Callaghan and Stull, faced to the wall, became a rasping monotony. Rowdy counted as sheaf after sheaf of currency went into the sack, and when there was forty thousand, he took the sack from Buckmaster's hand.

"Thanks," Rowdy said.

"You'll never get away with this!" Buckmaster snapped, his lips drawn thin. "I've told you that. You'll be hunted to the ends of the earth!"

"Now don't you fret about me," Rowdy said. "Here." Dropping the sack to the floor, he dug into a pocket with his free hand and produced the china stallion he'd carried since the night its worthlessness had been revealed in John Crenshaw's bedroom. Tossing the tiny figurine toward Buckmaster, Rowdy said, "This is something for you, to make up your loss. Fellow that gave it to me said it was worth one hundred thousand dollars. That puts you sixty thousand to the good."

Buckmaster instinctively plucked the stallion from the air and stood staring at it. Rowdy said, "I'll be leaving now. You boys stay here. After I get out of the house, I'm going to Injun around for a spell. Maybe I'll be outside for five minutes. Maybe an hour. The point is that you can't be sure how long. The only thing you can be sure about is that the first one of you who pokes his nose outside is going to stop a bullet if I'm still around."

Then he was backing up the stairs, the gunny sack in his left hand, the gun in his right. But once to the top of the steps, he silently closed the door and as silently fled down the hall toward the front door giving out of the house. That talk of lingering outside had been pure bluff, designed to keep Buckmaster and Callaghan and Stull from being too hasty in dashing in pursuit of him. Actually Rowdy was cherishing the minutes now, knowing he had none to spare if he were to get this money back to Latigo and into the hands of its proper owners before those same owners attacked Crenshaw's bank. It was for this last phase of his mission that he'd been saving himself and his horse, and, crossing the gallery, Rowdy vaulted its railing and lighted running, heading for the horse he'd left ground-anchored.

And that was when a man loomed up out of the sullen night, a man who'd just dismounted from a saddler and was stalking toward the house. Rowdy's first thought was that it was one of Stull's crew, but a sudden flare of lightning gave him a real look, and he recognised that stocky form and was recognised in turn. The thunder boomed as he got a grip on Butch Rafferty's arm, and Rowdy, vast surprise in his voice, said, "What in blazes are *you* doing here?"

"I've come," Butch Rafferty said flatly, "to look at a man through gunsmoke."

Rowdy said, "In there? In the Eyrie? I noticed you're packing a gun. Where did you get it?"

"Borrowed Stonehead Jackson's. You'd better get on your way, Dow. This is no affair of yours. Myra's gone to town looking for you. She tried to talk me out of this, and, failing, she left the schoolhouse and lit out after you. If I don't ride back from here, I'd take it kindly if you see that no harm comes to her."

All of this was one vast riddle to Rowdy Dow. His surprise at finding Rafferty here had been too sudden to allow clear thinking, and nothing Rafferty said added up to any sense. But Rowdy knew his own need all too well, and, his grip still on Rafferty, he shook the outlaw. "We can't stay here," Rowdy said quickly. "We're needed in Latigo—both of us, likely. John Crenshaw is forted up inside his bank, and Clee Drummond's with him. The basin ranchers were liquoring this morning and talking of storming that bank. It's a long story, and there's no time to tell it, but I've got the money in this sack that will get Crenshaw out of a tight. It's got to be delivered and delivered fast. Maybe it's too late now."

Rafferty's voice stayed flat and lifeless. "If Crenshaw needs siding, he can count on my gun. But not until I've finished my private chores. You'd better ride, Dow. I'm going inside."

"But why?" Rowdy demanded.

"Because of *this*," Rafferty said. "Can you see it in the dark? Stonehead Jackson showed it to me late this afternoon. And Stonehead admitted he got it out of yonder house—he was snooping around one day and picked it up when he was here with Stull's crew. Do you savvy what it means, Dow?"

The lightning flared again, and Rowdy found himself staring—staring in utter astonishment—at the object Butch Rafferty held in his open palm. For once again Rowdy was seeing the china stallion, only this couldn't be the china stallion, for he'd turned the figurine over to Thane Buckmaster as a grim joke not ten minutes before. But it was an exact duplicate of that little rearing horse, and even as Rowdy sensed the incredible truth, the darkness closed down again, and the thunder boomed, and Butch Rafferty had slipped away from him and was gone.

19. Through Gunsmoke

A MAN CAN THINK OF many things in a single second. And thus it was with Rowdy Dow as he stood alone in the rain-swept yard before the Eagle's Eyrie, his eyes searching the night in an attempt to locate Butch Rafferty. For Rowdy faced a choice, and all the factors that went into the making of that choice thronged through his mind, turning this into the bleakest moment he had ever known.

There was John Crenshaw to remember—John Crenshaw who was beleaguered in his own bank down in distant Latigo and who might be saved by the money Rowdy now held in the sack in his hand. Rowdy had outlawed himself to get that money; he had played against the odds and won, but his coup was not complete until the money was delivered into the proper hands. In a sense, Rowdy's mission in the basin, beclouded at times by many complications, had been to help John Crenshaw. But that had not been for Crenshaw's sake alone, but for Butch Rafferty's, for Rafferty had wanted to make amends for the harm he had unwittingly done this same John Crenshaw.

And so Rowdy came around a mental circle and back to Butch Rafferty and to the ancient debt he owed Rafferty. That debt would be paid in full if Rafferty came out of this affair alive and free, and Clee Drummond had intimated that a pardon for the veteran owlhooter was a possibility. But Rafferty had risked his chance at true freedom by scaling Deer Lodge's wall, and Rafferty would jeopardise the pardon beyond redemption if he looked at a man through gunsmoke. And that was exactly what Rafferty was on his way to do; he'd said so himself. There was much that Rowdy didn't understand—the desperate urge that had driven Rafferty here through the storm—that duplicate china stallion Rafferty clutched in his hand. But if ever there'd been a man with homicide in his heart, it was Butch Rafferty to-night.

It was that picture of Butch Rafferty as Rowdy had last seen him in the lightning's flare—eyes wild and hand thrust forward—that made Rowdy's decision for him, for suddenly the problem had resolved itself into simpler terms. John Crenshaw needed help, true, but Crenshaw's greatest danger was in having his life's work wrecked before his eyes. Butch Rafferty's need was greater, for Rafferty's life might be forfeit in yonder brooding house. Three men were there—three men who were doubtless at this very moment seeking guns and hurrying to take Rowdy's trail. And Butch Rafferty was going to find the odds against him when he came stampeding inside.

And so thinking, Rowdy was sprinting back toward the house. Reaching the gallery steps, he placed the gunny sack at the foot of them and came charging to the door, and, just as he reached the portal, he was certain that gun-thunder reverberated beyond it. Easing the door open, he slipped inside and closed it after him and found the hallway dark as a mole's dream of disaster. Either the lamp was no longer burning in that high-ceilinged living-room where he'd bearded Thane Buckmaster not so very long ago, or else the door to that room was closed.

Gun in hand, Rowdy took a cautious step forward. The acrid odour of powdersmoke was heavy in the air. Rowdy thought he perceived dim movement down the hall, and he tilted his gun but he stayed his hand; if a man lurked in the darkness it might be Butch Rafferty. The veteran owlhooter hadn't been more than a minute ahead of Rowdy—that stunning minute while Rowdy had stood in the yard debating. Flattened against the wall, Rowdy began inching along, and he almost collided with a hall-tree which stood there.

The hall-tree was big and heavy, and Rowdy had seen it before without actually being conscious of it. From it was suspended what felt to Rowdy's touch as though it might be Thane Buckmaster's cape, and Rowdy was inspired. Feeling his way to the bottom of the garment, Rowdy got a grip on it and then stepped to the opposite wall, tugging at the cape as he did. The hall-tree tipped over with a tremendous crash, and, in the same instant, there was a louder roar as a gun spoke from down the hallway. A bullet cut the air dangerously close to Rowdy's head, the lead thunking into the closed door at the end of the hall. But the gunflash had given Rowdy a brief glimpse of the contorted face of Curly Bill Callaghan. And now boots reverberated as Callaghan stampeded up the stairs to the second storey.

Rowdy had learned what he'd wanted to know—the identity of the dim figure he'd seen. And, remembering the one shot he'd been certain he'd heard as he'd crossed the gallery, he could picture what had happened here. The three he'd left in the underground room—Buckmaster, Callaghan and Stull—had likely spent a few moments waiting to be sure that he, Rowdy, had gone from the house. Then they'd ventured upstairs, their intent being to quickly get their hands on the guns Rowdy had taken from them and dropped in that high-ceilinged living-room. Since Callaghan now had a gun, it followed that the three had reached weapons. Probably they'd all come into the hallway, guns in hands, just as Butch Rafferty had charged into the house. Rafferty had then fired the shot Rowdy had heard, and someone among the three had been quick-witted enough to dash back into the big living-room and douse the lamp. Then the three had spread out in the darkness, hoping either to close in on Rafferty or to elude him. Most likely it had been every man for himself.

All of which meant that five men were in this house, all of them armed and playing a desperate game of blindman's buff with everybody "it" and hot lead to do the tagging. Buckmaster and his allies had the advantage of knowing the house, though Bat Stull, likely, was not too familiar with it. But Stull was the least of Rowdy's worries. And, since Callaghan had gone upstairs, Rowdy darted after him. Every man to his own meat at a time like this.

Up until now, Rowdy had borne no definite grudge against Buckmaster's foreman. He had never liked the hard and petulant look of Callaghan, and he'd truly earned Callaghan's hatred to-night when he'd forced the fellow, along with Buckmaster and Stull, to lock-step to the underground vault. But Callaghan had sided Buckmaster in all the scheming, and that made the man as unscrupulous as his master. And there'd been something altogether too personal about that

bullet that had buzzed through the darkness a moment ago.
It was kill or be killed, and that left Rowdy little choice.

The thunder boomed again as Rowdy hit the stairs, and
he took the steps two at a time under cover of that explo-
sion. Remembering the light in the barn when he'd first
approached the Eyrie, Rowdy blessed the storm and hoped
that the thick walls of this house were also helping keep the
sounds of this fracas from reaching Stull's men who were
undoubtedly in the barn. There were at least three men out
there, now that Stonehead Jackson had quit the bunch, and
perhaps the tally was five, if the two who'd been holding
the herd in that hidden ravine had joined the others. Rowdy
wasn't anxious to have the odds increased to any greater than
they were.

At the head of the stairs, Rowdy paused. Now he was
facing down another dark hallway with doors giving off from
it. These doors, he supposed, led into bedrooms. Butch
Rafferty and his daughter had been confined on this second
storey during their captivity, and Clee Drummond had also
reported being in this part of the house during his brief stay
in the Eyrie. Sucking in a long breath, Rowdy tip-toed
forward. Callaghan was up here somewhere. Had Callaghan
dodged into one of the rooms? And if so, which one? Very
carefully Rowdy made his way the length of the hall,
encountering no one. Again he paused, every nerve alert, his
eyes and ears straining, and, at that moment, a gun sounded
from somewhere far below—a shot, and then two other
closely-spaced shots hard on the heels of the first.

Downstairs, of course. Either Rafferty had closed with
quarry somewhere in this vast building, or had himself been
cornered. But now the silence was thick again, broken only
by the wild drumming of rain on the roof over Rowdy's
head. Within Rowdy grew a frantic urge to get downstairs
again, to investigate those shots, but Callaghan was still
about, and Callaghan would constitute a menace as long as
the man walked free. Taking a step back toward the stairs,
Rowdy deliberately made a scuffing sound with his boots as
though he had stumbled over something in the darkness, and,
at the same time, he leaped quickly sideways.

It was a variation of the ruse he'd worked when he'd
tipped over the hall-tree, and it got the same results. A door
opened farther along the hall and an orange streak of

gunflame lanced across the darkness in the direction of the sound Rowdy had made. Again Rowdy felt the hot breath of a bullet. Then the door was slammed shut, but Rowdy had located Curly Bill Callaghan.

Hugging the wall, Rowdy inched toward that door. Keeping his back to the wall, he paused just short of the door and, reaching, got his hand on the knob. Slowly turning the knob, he bent his wrist and shoved the door inward, quickly withdrawing his hand with almost the same motion. Again Callaghan's gun spoke, the bullet thudding into a door across the hall. After that there was silence, heavy and ominous. Callaghan, somewhere within the open room, didn't dare venture close enough to the door to close it.

"You missed, Callaghan," Rowdy said, still keeping tight to the wall. "Better come out with your hands hoisted."

A throaty curse. Then: "Come in after me!" Callaghan challenged.

Rowdy shrugged. "I've no time to waste, Callaghan. But I haven't any special craving for your hide. Not if you want to play sensible. Drop your gun on the floor, and you can walk out of the room with no harm from me. What do you say?"

A minute trickled by, and another. Rowdy, his ears strained for any movement Callaghan might make, tried to sense the workings of the other's mind, and he pictured Callaghan weighing fear against belligerency and striving for a decision. Then: "I'm taking you at your word," Callaghan said, and something thudded to the floor.

Bending low, Rowdy turned on his heel and dived into the room. He had encountered treachery in this house before, and he expected it now, for, whatever Callaghan had dropped, it hadn't been a gun. Some object from a bureau top, likely, a heavy hair-brush perhaps. But Rowdy was through with stalling while the minutes slipped away; he had given this man his chance and Callaghan had abused it, and there was nothing left now but a flaming finish. Callaghan fired as Rowdy came lurching in. Rowdy felt the bullet pluck at his shirt sleeve, and he saw the frantic face of Buckmaster's foreman in the gunflash and knew that fear was in the man. Rowdy was firing as he came, but he'd waited that one split-second for Callaghan's shot and spotted the man, and

Callaghan doubled over, folding his arms across his chest as he went down.

He was dead when Rowdy bent to touch him, and Rowdy didn't linger after that. Coming out of the room and along the hallway to the stairs, he eased down the steps as silently as he could. Buckmaster and Stull were still within the house, and both might be alive, and that made a need for wariness, but, at the same time, Rowdy was desperately eager to find Rafferty. Reaching the bottom of the stairs, he stood in the dark, ground-floor hallway for a moment listening, and then headed to the door leading to the subterranean vault. Wrenching the door open and stepping quickly aside, he saw lamp light below. And someone was down there.

"Rafferty——?" Rowdy whispered.

A man stirred. "That you, Dow?"

Rowdy descended, and he came into the underground room to find a lamp burning on the table and a man sprawled dead upon the floor. Butch Rafferty stood swaying on his feet, a gun lying on the table near him while the grey-faced outlaw, his shirt stripped away, attempted to tie a pad in place over his ribs. Rowdy glanced at the dead man. "Buckmaster," he said and reached Rafferty's side. "I heard the shots. You hard hit, Butch?"

"Not much more than a scratch," said Rafferty, and the wildness was gone from his eyes. "But I've lost blood. Here, help me tie this thing, I found the lamp here after I cornered yonder carrion and shot it out with him. Risked lighting it so I could see what I was doing. I heard shots, too. You get yourself a wolf?"

"Callaghan," Rowdy said, and made his fingers busy with the crude bandage. "Stull's still loose, I guess, but he's probably hiding under a bed. We'd better get out of here in a hurry."

"Yes," said Rafferty. "The chores are about finished."

Awkwardly getting into the tattered remnant of his shirt, the old owlhooter groped into a pocket and produced an article. It was that china stallion, the one he'd showed Rowdy in the yard, the duplicate to the figurine Rowdy had carried so far. Taking a step toward Buckmaster's sprawled form, Rafferty dropped the stallion upon the dead man. "That," said Rafferty, "finishes out a long circle." And there was something about his words and the gesture that had preceded them that made the mystery no longer a mystery to Rowdy.

"You're harder hit than you pretend," Rowdy said. "Too hard hit to sit a saddle, maybe. And we've got to get to Latigo fast. Come on. We'll help ourselves to that fancy rig of Buckmaster's."

Blowing out the lamp, he got an arm around Rafferty and helped the oldster up the stairs. In the ground-floor hallway Rowdy paused for a moment, listening intently, but the house was silent again, and even the thunder seemed to be growing more distant. But Rowdy hadn't taken a half-dozen steps along the hall when he paused, stiffening.

"What is it?" Rafferty demanded.

"The front door!" Rowdy said quickly. "It's open. Feel the draught? I closed the door when I came in, and I'll swear it was still closed when I came down from the second floor a few minutes ago. Do you see what it means?"

"Stull——?" Rafferty guessed.

"He's grabbed a chance to get out of the house," Rowdy judged. "That means he's headed for the barn to gather his men. They'll be blocking our way as we try to leave here."

"Take your arm from around me, and keep your gun-hand free," Rafferty counselled. "I'll do likewise. We ain't going to be stopped now!"

20. The Road to Latigo

WHEN THEY CAME CAUTIOUSLY out of the house, Rowdy found the money sack where he'd left it at the foot of the gallery steps. Stull's departure, then, had been so hasty that the man hadn't stumbled upon the currency. A quick, whispered consultation with Rafferty told Rowdy that most of his surmising had been right. Rafferty had come into the Eyrie to find Buckmaster, Callaghan and Stull grouped in the hall. Rafferty's first shot had sent the three scattering. One man had darted into the high-ceilinged living-room and extinguished the lamp. That had been Stull, Rowdy guessed, and Stull had remained hidden in the room while death stalked the house.

And now Stull had seen his opportunity and slipped outside. That suggested all manner of potentialities, none of them good, and Rowdy had another concern as well. Rafferty, unsupported as they emerged, had lurched heavily against Rowdy several times. Rafferty had lost a great deal of blood, and, in the old owlhooter's present condition, he was apt to be more of a handicap than a help if another fight shaped up. And there'd be a fight. For Stull, the game had played itself out in Latigo Basin to-night; the man had hitched his wagon to Thane Buckmaster's star, and that star had gone crashing. Stull would be desperately determined not to leave empty-handed.

Coming around the house, Rowdy kept the gunny sack in his left hand, a gun ready in his right. The rain had slackened to a mere whisper, the thunder sounded remote, and the lightning flashes were feeble and far between. Rafferty staggering along beside him, the two came warily, but the yard was deserted. Rowdy made out the dim shape of an open wagon shed, and from it protruded Buckmaster's fancy surrey. "Better forget about the rig," Rafferty said. "Those matched blacks are likely in the barn, and I can see lantern shine through the cracks. That's where Stull's headed."

"And that's where I'm going," Rowdy declared. "You get to a barn window and cover me. We need that surrey mighty bad."

Easing toward the barn, Rowdy found its big door open wide enough to admit a man, and when he cautiously peered inside he saw that the lower floor was empty. A lantern burned smokily upon a box, and horses stomped in the stalls, and Rowdy's eyes searched out a ladder at the far end—a ladder leading to the hayloft where Stull's men had undoubtedly bedded down for the night, unaware of the ruckus in the big house beyond.

Into the barn, Rowdy hugged the shadows, and he heard Stull's voice then, high and excited. Stull was in the loft. "Buckmaster's dead and so's Callaghan," he was saying. "I stood at the head of the stairs above the cellar, and I heard Rafferty talking. Dow was with him."

Someone made a remark that was incoherent to Rowdy, and Stull spoke again. "Of course there's more dinero left in the vault! Dow only took forty thousand. But Buckmaster's dead, I tell you, and he knew the combination. It will take blasting powder and time and the proper tools to open that vault, and we haven't got those things. But there's forty thousand in Dow's gunny sack. We can get that before he gets away from here."

They came spilling down the ladder, Stull first and the others stumbling after him, and Rowdy waited until they'd all reached the barn's floor, counting heads as they came. Six of them. That meant that the two who'd been holding the stolen herd had returned to the Eyrie, as he'd guessed. When they stood grouped at the foot of the ladder, Rowdy spoke from the shadows. "Hoist your hands!" he barked. "All of you!"

Someone cursed, and there was furtive movement among them, but glass suddenly shattered explosively as a gun-barrel came thrusting through a window set in the rear wall. Rafferty's voice filled the barn. "Stand your hands!" Rafferty advised. "I can see every man. The first one who twitches is the first to die!"

They stood then transfixed, their hands hoisted and hate in their eyes, and Rowdy smiled grimly. "One of you help yourself to that lariat on yonder peg and tie Bat's hands behind him," he said. "*Get at it!* There, that's better. Do a good job, now."

It was Luke, of the low hairline, who'd obeyed, and when Bat seemed adequately trussed, Rowdy moved forward and examined the knots. Then he carefully lifted six-shooters from holsters and tossed the guns into an empty stall. "Come along, boys," he urged his prisoners. "One of you pick up the lantern. The rest can get harness onto those two fancy blacks."

They obeyed sullenly, their sharp glances moving alternately from Rowdy to that rear window where Butch Rafferty had posted himself. The blacks harnessed, Rowdy backed to the barn door and slid it wide and then ordered the group outside and to the wagon shed. He kept them bunched, and, as they fastened the team to the surrey, Rafferty came around the barn. Rowdy said, "You'll find my saddler over by yonder bushes. Fetch him and tie him to the back of this rig, Butch. We'll leave your cayuse here. Crenshaw can pick him up later."

Rafferty went off into the darkness, and Rowdy said, "A couple of you boys boost Stull into the back seat of this rig. There, that's fine." Rafferty shaped up out of the night, trailing a horse behind him, and he tied the saddler to the surrey. Rowdy had examined the harness to be sure it was properly fastened, and now he climbed into the surrey and took the reins, Rafferty lumbering up after him. Rowdy grinned down at Stull's men who stood watching. "Adios, gents," Rowdy said. "When you take our trail, don't crowd us too close. We'll be heading to Latigo where the law's waiting for you, and Bat will be with us. Start throwing lead, and you might hit him."

Stull found quavering voice. "You fellows stay here, savvy! It's *me* that's in a split stick!"

Rowdy got the whip and cracked it, and the surrey lurched forward. Aiming it through the trees, Rowdy came out upon the trail that tilted downward, and he lifted the horses to a high run, heedless of the dangers of curve and slant. "They know we're packing money," Rowdy said. "They'll give us a run. But maybe Bat's being with us will slow 'em. It was the best I could do.''

Butch Rafferty made no reply. He had stood vigil at the barn window and thus enabled Rowdy to accomplish this coup, but the old outlaw had carried himself this far by sheer will power. For Rafferty was leaning heavily against Rowdy's shoulder now; he had fainted.

Rowdy had to give his attention to the trail. He took curves on two wheels and wrung cries of anguish and fear from Bat Stull, and he almost piled them up more than once. Rafferty recovered consciousness, mumbling incoherently. Rowdy paid little heed to him. He was measuring the minutes, deciding how long it would take Stull's bunch to recover their guns and get into saddles, and he wished now that he'd rounded up all the horses at Buckmaster's place and driven them into the timber. But he'd needed time; he was still acutely aware that every minute lost was a minute more it would take him to get to Latigo, and he'd made as much compromise as he could. But as fleet as this surrey was, saddlers would be fleeter. His only hope was to gain a margin that would put him so near to Latigo by the time pursuit overtook him that Stull's men would lose their courage and turn back.

Whether the fetching of Bat Stull would be an advantage remained to be seen. Taking the man had been an impulse, but now Rowdy wasn't so sure it had been a wise one. He remembered the night in the schoolhouse when he'd aroused the suspicions of Stull's men against Bat, and he knew there was no real affection in the outfit. They clung together out of necessity, but whether the danger of the one would be the concern of the others was debatable. It was that forty thousand dollars that would fetch the pursuit. They had come to the basin with high hopes; they had outlawed themselves in an effort to lay their hands upon easy money. To-night they'd be remembering that there was this one last chance of saving their mission from complete failure.

The surrey was still intact as it roared past the schoolhouse; those matched blacks of Buckmaster's had taken this trail often, and it was their instinct as well as Rowdy's skill that had kept the rig from disaster on the slant. The schoolhouse was dark, and likely deserted unless Stonehead Jackson still remained there. Down upon the basin floor,

Rowdy found that it had ceased raining; the moon was trying to finger its way through the clouds. From all the sign, the storm had been less severe here than in the hills. Rowdy drew to a stop then, resting the blacks and begrudging the minutes, and he alighted and scanned the backtrail. Maybe Stull's men had decided to try forcing Buckmaster's vault, futile as their efforts might be. But shortly Rowdy made out dim movement to the rear, and when he put an ear to the ground, he heard the rumble of hooves.

Stull's men were coming. Leaping into the surrey, Rowdy took the reins and plied the whip. Bouncing and jostling over the wagon road, Rowdy put everything into the race, but soon guns were banging behind him. The distance was too great to make a six-shooter dangerous, but panic surged again in Bat Stull. "Stop the rig!" he shouted. "Do you want us all to get shot?"

"Shut up!" Rowdy barked.

He was worried about his saddler. The horse still thundered along behind the surrey, and if a chance shot brought the mount down and the tie-rope to the rig held, there could be disaster. He'd fetched the horse for a purpose; if the pursuit crowded too close he'd intended turning the reins over to Rafferty, and, taking to the saddler, hold off Stull's men while Rafferty toted the money on to town. But Rafferty was in no shape to handle the rig, and Rowdy couldn't risk the time now to free the saddler. Onward they roared. Once the surrey struck a large rock in the road and bounced high, and Rowdy expected a shattered wheel. But the rig held together, and the miles blurred past, and still those guns barked behind them.

Rowdy had lost track of time and distance. His eyes on the road, hands tight on the reins, he was intent only upon maintaining this tremendous pace. Sometimes he thrust his head from the surrey and had a look behind, and always saw the red, winking eyes of gun-flashes. Rafferty aroused himself and laboriously scrambled to the rear seat of the rig. Shoving Stull to one side, the veteran owlhooter levelled his six-shooter, and, firing over Rowdy's saddler, helped keep the pursuit at a distance.

Then, suddenly, they were into the broken country, the road dropping down into coulees and skirting bluffs, and Stull's men were lost from view. Rounding a turn, the lights of Latigo sprang before them, and Rafferty heaved a long sigh and said, "Easy now, Rowdy. We've shaken them. The last look I got, the whole bunch seemed to be turning back."

Bat Stull had taken to cursing in a monotonous, strident voice; he was a man who had watched hope shape out of disaster and then seen that hope fade away. But still Rowdy plied the whip, and he came wheeling into Latigo and up the main street, the blacks foam-flecked and the trail-battered surrey looking like something held together by haywire. Then Rowdy found his passage blocked, and he brought the surrey to a skidding stop, for the street before Crenshaw's bank was choked with men, a heaving, surging mob that filled the way from one boardwalk to another.

Coming down out of the rig, Rowdy helped Rafferty to a stand and then dragged Stull from the surrey and propelled him across the courthouse lawn. Over yonder, by the cannon, Rowdy had made out two familiar figures, and, nearing them, he tripped Stull and spilled the man to the ground. "Here's Stull, Pickens," he told the waiting sheriff. "You can lock him up till Logan MacLean prefers charges. And here's Butch Rafferty. Get him down to Doc Pettibone's as fast as you can. Me and Stumpy can handle things meanwhile."

Stumpy Grampis had sent up a wild "*Yipp-ee-ee!*" at sight of Rowdy, but the sound was almost lost in the many-throated roar from the group that surged before the bank. Out of that clamour Rowdy distinguished coherent words. "Open up, Crenshaw! Give us what you've got left before you lose that for us, too!"—"Open up, mister, or we'll tear the bank apart!" But still the door remained closed, the shades drawn.

Sheriff Slim Pickens, his Adam's apple bobbing in astonishment at Rowdy's sudden arrival, had recovered his wits and recognised the most urgent need. Already he was leading Butch Rafferty off down the street in the direction of Doc Pettibone's cottage. Rowdy said, "Looks like I got back in time, Stumpy. But that mob's about ready to make big trouble."

"It started raining here after you left this morning," Stumpy said. "That sort of dampened the ranchers' ardour, so to speak, but it likewise kept them in the saloons and at their drinking. They started drifting down to the bank about a half-hour ago. Crenshaw knows there's no sense trying to talk to them. Me and Pickens has been standing by, ready to take a hand once they get rough."

"Here's their money," Rowdy said, and indicated the gunny sack.

Someone in the mob made his voice heard above the rest. "Let's get a battering ram and bust in the door!" he shouted, and the idea was avidly seized by a group who went lurching away to make a search. Stumpy frowned and said, "How you gonna make that bunch listen to you? They're raising such a rumpus they can't even hear 'emselves think. It would take this cannon to get their attention."

"Cannon——?" said Rowdy and turned to look at the piece on the courthouse lawn. He knew as little about cannons as he'd known about ascension balloons, but he'd seen the shape of inspiration. "Stumpy, if we could find someone who knows how to fire this overgrown horse pistol ——!"

"Shucks," said Stumpy, "I can fire the danged thing. Used to haul freight into Fort Benton, and I've watched the sojers a heap of times. I'll need powder and a few other things and——"

"Run and see if the mercantile store is still open," Rowdy urged, all excitement now. "They'll have powder."

Stumpy was off with alacrity, and Rowdy had nothing to do but watch and wait. The mob still made its clamour, and eventually men returned to it, bearing what appeared to be a wagon tongue, and he saw those men work their way through the jostling crowd, trying to reach the door. There were saner heads among the mob, for someone kept crying, "Take it easy, boys! We don't want to bust up property. All we want is our money."

Rowdy glanced anxiously down the street. Then Stumpy appeared, bearing a partially filled keg of powder, a long piece of oilcloth, apparently torn for a counter, and a ten-inch length of stiff wire. "Lend a hand, partner," Stumpy ordered, and the two fell to work, Rowdy taking his cue from the other. Fingers busy, Stumpy used his pocket knife to cut squares from the oilcloth, and into these he poured powder from the keg. Each load of powder wrapped and tied with strips of oilcloth, Stumpy fitted them into the mouth of the cannon. A ramming rod was held by hooks under the piece, and with this Stumpy shoved the oilcloth containers deep into the barrel until they fitted snugly against the breech. "Need some wadding," he declared. "Paper or cloth will do."

Rowdy had darted off. Bat Stull had gotten to his feet and was about to run away, and Rowdy tripped him again. Slim Pickens came panting across the lawn, his eyes a pair of question marks, and Rowdy said, "Here, sit on this jigger!" Then Rowdy turned back to his partner. "Here's wadding for you," Rowdy said and dug into the gunny sack. "We won't only use the cannon to get attention. We'll make it speak a lingo these gents will like!"

And so currency was stuffed into the cannon, and the sweat was dripping from Stumpy Grampis as he took the piece of stiff wire and rammed it down into the firing-hole, working it until he'd punctured a hole through the oilcloth load beneath. A handful of powder filled the firing-hole, and Stumpy began working the elevating screw until he had the cannon tilted at a forty-five degree angle. Drawing a match across his trousers, he touched it to the firing-hole.

"Plug yore ears, Rowdy," he advised. "Here goes."

It was as though the earth itself had suddenly exploded. The burst of powder-flame lighted the night like a thousand lanterns, and, across the way, the men who'd reached the bank door with the battering ram and were in the act of wielding it, suddenly froze. Through the billowing smoke, Rowdy saw men turning, their mouths agape, their faces lifted. Then paper was showering down upon them, and someone, turned suddenly sober, was crying, "*Greenbacks! My gawd, it's raining greenbacks!*"

Rowdy cupped his hands to his mouth. "The rest of your money is over here. John Crenshaw will pass it to you. Here he comes now." For the bank door had burst open and Crenshaw and Clee Drummond stepped into view, and even at this distance Rowdy could see that Crenshaw was smiling.

Rowdy sighed, a long and weary but satisfied sigh. Turning to Pickens, he said, "You'd better get up off Stull and tote him to jail. And if you get a fast posse to riding, you can likely round up Stull's men. Shouldn't be surprised if some of those ranchers who were hankering to tear down Crenshaw's bank and who are now busy rooting under the boardwalks for greenbacks would ride with you."

"I'll nail 'em," Pickens promised. "Ever since I first

heard Butch Rafferty was in the basin, I've had deputies posted atop Latigo Pass. Stull's men can't get away.''

Bat Stull, hauled to his feet by the sheriff, said, "I ain't going to jail alone! You got to lock up Rowdy Dow and Butch Rafferty, too. They did murder to-night, Sheriff. Go up to the Eagle's Eyrie and have a look if you don't believe me!''

Pickens said, ''Is that right, Dow?''

Rowdy shrugged. ''I got Callaghan, yes. It was him or me, and you can't jail a man for self-defence. And Butch Rafferty nailed Thane Buckmaster. But all you can do about that is pin a rose on Butch, Slim. And hand him a reward. You see, Thane Buckmaster was wanted dead or alive back in Ashland, Ohio. They knew him as Sam Buckner in his home town. Another name he went by was Sam Usher. Don't look so flabbergasted, Slim. It's a long story, and when the chores are finished I'll tell it to you over a drink.''

21. When Friends Bend Elbows

THEY MET ALONG LATIGO's main street in the late afternoon after each had put in a busy day in his own fashion, and, by common consent, they came trooping into the nearest saloon and bellied up to the bar. They stood there shoulder to shoulder, two badge-toters and two men who'd ridden the owlhoot, and Rowdy, anticipating the wants of all, signalled the barkeep and said, "Four whiskies."

"You can pour me four, likewise," said Stumpy Grampis.

"One apiece," Rowdy said firmly. "We had our spree in Jubilee, remember."

Clee Drummond had donned his shield-shaped United States marshal's badge once again, and he gave Sheriff Slim Pickens a congratulatory slap on the back that nearly caved in that thin lawman's chest. The whisky bottle came sliding along the bar and four glasses followed it, and Stumpy levelled off a drink that would have sent a grizzly bear somersaulting backward. The glasses hoisted, Drummond said, "Here's to full jail-houses and solvent banks."

"They're comin' hand in hand these days," Pickens conceded when the drinks had been downed. "Bagged every man of Stull's outfit early this morning. They were up at the Eyrie trying to hammer the dial off that vault in Buckmaster's cellar. The vault will be opened legal-like once I get around to it. And there's no argument but what John Crenshaw will get one hundred thousand dollars out of whatever is left in that vault."

"He won't really need it," Rowdy said. "Not like he's been needing it, anyway. I was out to Crenshaw's ranch this

161

morning, Slim. Helped move Butch Rafferty there from Doc Pettibone's place. More danged ranchers showed up with sheepish looks on their faces to shake Crenshaw's hand than you could shoot a cannon at. That blast last night really blew some sense into 'em.''

"Pettibone says Rafferty should be in shape to ride in a week or so," Stumpy said.

"And I got a letter off to the governor this noon," Drummond said. "It sort of paints up Rafferty as the hero of Latigo Basin. Some of the things that you and Stumpy did, Dow, I pinned onto Butch to make the picture better. Reckon you boys understand. There'll be a pardon, or there'll be a petition signed by every Latigo rancher, I'm betting.''

"The governor is mighty leery of petitions," Rowdy said reminiscently. "By the way, Drummond, did you get a chance to speak to Crenshaw about Stonehead Jackson, like I asked you to last night after the excitement died down?''

Drummond nodded. "Crenshaw's got a job for the big galoot, and he sent one of his boys to the schoolhouse to rope and tie him. Don't know what kind of cowhand Jackson will make, but he shore ought to keep the boys entertained in the bunkhouse.''

"Speaking of entertainment," Slim Pickens said, "I clipped a coupon out of a magazine the other night. An outfit sells a correspondence course which teaches you how to throw your voice. Claims it will make a feller a howling success at church socials and such. Which reminds me, I'll have to start watching for the mail train again.''

Stumpy sighed. "It's been a mighty long time between drinks," he observed pointedly.

The bottle went from hand to hand, and Stumpy poured himself enough to bring a steer to its knees. Hoisting the glass, he said, "I've got most of the pieces of the puzzle now, but there's still one thing that just doesn't fit. How in thunder did Thane Buckmaster live here in the basin without folks catching on that he was their ex-neighbour, Sam Usher?''

"It's simple enough," said Clee Drummond. "I've got most of the pieces, too, after talking to Rowdy and John Crenshaw and Butch Rafferty. Sam Buckner, which was the gent's right name, was the black sheep of a good family back in Ohio. He murdered a man years ago, then lit out for the West and took up a bit of land in Latigo Basin. While he was here, he was a seedy specimen, and he kept pretty much to himself. He made one slight mistake in those days, though. He came to Crenshaw's bank and asked for a loan, and he let the name of his home town slip out. Naturally he didn't want to be checked up on back in Ashland. But the town stuck in John Crenshaw's mind, and that was why Pickens, here, was able to wire the Acme people and get the story of Sam Buckner who'd turned himself into Sam Usher.''

"Buckner had a criminal streak in him a mile wide,'' Rowdy observed. "Small wonder he was willing enough to have his place used as a relay station by Butch Rafferty.''

"And Rafferty only saw him twice—as Sam Usher,'' Drummond went on. "Once when Rafferty made the dicker to get the grub and a change of horses at Usher's place, and again when Rafferty fetched the hundred thousand dollars to Usher. Both meetings were by lamplight, and Buckner was whiskered in those days, so it's no wonder that Butch didn't recognise Thane Buckmaster as the man who'd double-crossed him years ago.''

"And double-cross him he did,'' said Rowdy. "Not only did Buckner run away with the hundred thousand, but he tipped off the law as to which trail Rafferty had taken. That was how Rafferty came to end up in stony lonesome.''

"And Buckner, or Usher, hit the grit,'' said Stumpy. "That's plain enough. But he could have gone any place. Why did he circle back to Latigo Basin?''

"That's one of the pieces we'll have to guess at,'' said Drummond. "Buckner was money mad, and he wanted to make that hundred thousand grow. He had a big advantage in the basin; he knew the lie of the land from having lived here as a two-bit squatter. He knew what was worth investing in, and what was better left alone. To the basin people he was an outsider, a greenhorn. Actually he was wiser than any of them.''

"But I still can't savvy why they didn't recognise him!'' Stumpy reiterated.

"What do you remember about a man?'' Drummond countered. "The shape of his nose? The colour of his eyes?'' Drummond shook his head. "I'll bet you the price of a drink that you can't tell me exactly how John Crenshaw looks. No, it's personality that's remembered, and Buckner was careful, when he turned himself into Thane Buckmaster, to be as different from Sam Usher as he could possibly be. Where once he'd been seedy, he took to being neat. Even the cape was part of his act. And remember that he had the money to furnish himself with an entirely different background. Likely when basin folks first met him they felt there was something familiar about him, just as when you meet a stranger you often sense that he reminds you of someone you can't quite place. But as time went on, folks became more and more used to Thane Buckmaster, and all the while Sam Usher was growing dimmer in their memories. They just couldn't make any mental tie-up between the Eagle's Eyrie— the big house that Buckner built so he could look down upon the basin he intended to own—and the cheap shack he'd once lived in.''

"Callaghan must have known the truth," Rowdy surmised. "Crenshaw says that Buckner brought Curly Bill with him when Buckner came back to the basin as Thane Buckmaster.''

"There was probably another reason why Buckner returned to Latigo," Drummond judged. "Buckner's one great fear was of the man he'd double-crossed, Butch Rafferty. But if Rafferty ever got out of stony lonesome and took the trail of Buckner, or Usher, Butch would have expected it to lead *away* from the basin, not back to it.''

"And it was Rafferty's escaping that kicked over the cracker barrel," Rowdy said. "Buckner had things just about as he wanted them. He'd bided his time and played careful; he'd poisoned folks against John Crenshaw and got them borrowing money from him. Then he discovered that the railroad was building into the basin, and he was ready to close in for the kill. But, on the train coming back to Latigo, he saw Butch Rafferty disguised as a woman. Buckner told me himself that he recognised Butch when the hat and veil jarred off. That must have been a mighty bad moment for him.''

"So bad that he got stampeded," Drummond put in. "There could be no safety for him as long as Rafferty roamed free. So he kidnapped Rafferty and Myra out of the hotel and took them to the Eyrie. He could have turned

Rafferty over to the law, of course, and had Butch sent back to Deer Lodge, but as long as Rafferty was alive, Buckner was shaking in his boots. Rafferty had escaped the pen once, and he might escape again. So it must have been Buckmaster's plan that Rafferty was never to leave the Eyrie alive. But Buckmaster had to wait until the sign was right before he killed Butch.''

"Meanwhile, I paid two visits to the Eyrie," Rowdy said. "Slim, here, was along the first time. Myra lied and saved Buckner, and it's mighty plain now why she did. Then I went back to get Rafferty into the hills before Slim came with a posse. Buckner let me take Rafferty, because that suited him fine. His plan was to let Rafferty leave the Eyrie and then shoot him afterwards—as an escaped convict. He tried mighty hard to catch Butch in his sights the other day when Buckner's bunch chased us down out of the hills. But we fooled him.''

"And then Stonehead Jackson shook loose of Stull's bunch," said Stumpy, who was beginning to see the light. "And Jackson came to the schoolhouse where Butch was hiding. While Jackson had been at the Eyrie, he'd picked up a china stallion. In his thick head there was only *one* china stallion, and he figgered he was grabbing something valuable. When he remembered the stallion again and got around to showing it to Rafferty, old Butch must have just about gone through the ceiling. 'Cause it was a duplicate of the one all the fuss had been over.''

"Rafferty saw the truth then," Rowdy said. "You see, that night he'd snatched a china stallion from a shelf in Sam Usher's shack, telling Usher he'd send the stallion back as a token when he wanted the loot, there'd been *two* such stallions on Usher's shelf. Since the extra one had turned up in Buckmaster's house, it started Butch's mind to working and suddenly he saw the truth, just as I guessed it when Butch dropped the stallion on Buckner as he lay dead. Thane Buckmaster was Sam Usher. And that was why Butch had come up the hill with blood in his eye and paid off Buckner in the kind of coin he deserved.''

Slim Pickens wrinkled his brow. "Now you've got *me* puzzled," he confessed. "Why did Buckner hang onto the second stallion—the one thing that branded him as Sam Usher?''

"There could be only one reason," said Rowdy. "His old fear that Butch Rafferty might someday cross his trail. He was taking a chance that Butch hadn't noticed there were two stallions long ago. If Butch showed up, demanding the loot, Buckner was going to hand him the stallion and spin a yarn about having had it presented to him by a stranger who'd collected the loot. Remember, that was the idea of the stallion. It was to be a token that anybody could fetch. Obviously Buckner didn't keep the stallion out in plain sight at the Eyrie. Jackson was snooping around when he found it."

"I savvy," Pickens said.

"The china stallion should have put me wise to Buckmaster in the first place," Rowdy said. "Everybody in creation was trying to get their hands on that hoss. But when Buckmaster had Myra Rafferty at the Eyrie and I demanded the stallion, Buckmaster told her to give it to me. You see, Buckmaster was the one gent who wasn't interested in the stallion because he already had the one hundred thousand dollars it represented."

"And the case is closed," said Pickens. "I can't jail you, Rowdy, for taking money away from Buckner last night at gun-point. To-day I told Bat Stull that it might mean the shaving of a couple of years off the prison sentence he'll be getting if he talked up. He admitted that he clouted Crenshaw the other night and took the railroad beef money—at Buckmaster's orders. Restitution is no crime."

Clee Drummond said softly, "There's times when a fellow has to look at the shape of justice rather than the way the laws are written in the book. You're free to ride."

"And our horses are outside," said Rowdy.

Stumpy looked longingly at the unemptied bottle upon the bar, but Rowdy got him by the elbow. "See you fellows, later," said Rowdy and he urged his partner out to the hitch-rail where their horses waited. Stumpy had gotten his own saddler from the railroad that morning, and when the two swung aloft, Rowdy said, "We'll be hitting the trail. We can pick up our war-sack at the schoolhouse. I reckon it's still there. I don't like good-bys. We've seen our friends and drunk with those who were able to bend an elbow. It's the way to remember a man."

Stumpy said, "What about that thousand Clee Drummond

promised us for getting Rafferty's lost loot restored to Crenshaw?''

Smiling, Rowdy patted a pocket. "It's always embarrassing to ask a man for money. I slipped a thousand out of the gunny sack and into my pocket when I was loading the cannon last night. No sense in shooting away all the money in one evening."

Stumpy let out a whoop. "No toting water for railroad crews for us, even though Logan MacLean offered us a job this morning," he said. "We'll round-side in comfort this winter."

But when they'd put the town behind them and were wending along the wagon road toward Latigo Pass, Stumpy said, "Did you say good-by to Myra this morning?"

"Good-by?" Rowdy looked blank. "That girl was mighty busy, Stumpy. Didn't you know there's to be a wedding?"

Stumpy reined to an abrupt stop, a great suspicion in his eyes. "*A wedding!* Rowdy, you took a shine to that gal. I could see it plain. But, confound it, I figgered that you and me——"

"Easy," said Rowdy. "She's marrying Logan MacLean, not me. It was a case of love at first sight between those two, I reckon. Only, aboard the train, Myra had too much worry on her mind to be interested in romance. But when Rafferty lit out to look at Sam Buckner through gunsmoke last night, Myra headed for town to get me to stop him. She run into Logan MacLean and just fell into his arms, I guess. Shucks, what would she want with an ex-outlaw for a husband? She's got one for a father, and that's enough in the family. And we've given them a wedding present, Stumpy—Butch Rafferty's freedom. This morning I told Butch about the debt I'd owed him. The slate is clean."

Stumpy clutched at his saddlehorn. "We should have fetched along a bottle," he vowed. "I'm weak in the knees, pardner. For a minute I thought you was flinging me aside for a purty face!"

Rowdy smiled. They went jogging along then, stirrup to stirrup, and each turned sober with the reflection that their work here was finished. Behind them they would leave a basin from which the last shadow of trouble had been lifted. Behind them would be friends and the remembrance of a job well done. When they began climbing the pass, they would pause and sit their saddles for a while and have one last, long look, printing a picture of the tawny acres in their minds and in their hearts. And that they would take with them wherever their trail might lead.